Until Summer's End

Until Summer's End

VALERIE FLOURNOY

DOUBLEDAY & COMPANY, INC.
GARDEN CITY, NEW YORK
1986

For my special number one sister,
Celeste "Bernie" Flournoy, I dedicate
my first novel

All of the characters in this book
are fictitious, and any resemblance
to actual persons, living or dead,
is purely coincidental.

Library of Congress Cataloging-in-Publication Data

Flournoy, Valerie, 1952–
Until summer's end.

I. Title.
PS3556.L595U5   1986   813'.54   86-8808
ISBN 0-385-23391-4

Until Summer's End

CHAPTER ONE

A startling blue sky, peppered with billowy white clouds, confirmed another magnificent day and Brenna casually glanced east toward the coastline where a bevy of raucous sea gulls appeared to keep pace with her. She loved to drive so traveling through New York State en route to Ellsworth, Maine, had been both enjoyable and relaxing. Maine. The state was a slice of Americana, somehow able to maintain its original, old New England character. Brenna hadn't felt this stimulated or alive since she departed for her study abroad a year ago.

Every town and village Brenna drove through revealed a wealth of Early American architecture or simple scenic allure. Despite the barren stretch of roadway—Maine was by no means overpopulated—there was something about the countryside that appealed to her. Occasionally, a riotous assortment of spring buds dotted the roadside, breaking up the monotony of pebbled beaches and tall, scraggly grass. Scotch pines, hemlocks, and white and red spruces scented the air, once she turned off the coastal highway, fitting backdrops for the various animals and birds that crossed her path.

But the most breathtaking views were of the sea. The rocky coastline of Maine was vastly different from the sandy, south New Jersey beaches Brenna was accustomed to. White foamy waters pounded against seashells, while mighty cliffs stretched skyward from the sea depths. Brenna had fallen under the spell of the sparsely populated countryside, instilling her with the hope that her summer in Maine would not only be productive but restful, something she desperately craved after the past two months.

Brenna located the Winslow Boarding House without any difficulty and parked her forest-green Nissan in front of the building. She grabbed her purse, then stopped to view herself in the rearview mirror. Her brown hair—its reddish tones highlighted by the sun's setting rays—was mussed slightly from the breeze wafting through the open window. She had meant to change her clothes before meeting her new employer but, before she realized it, Ellsworth was upon her. The gravel marks on the seat of her formfitting tan linen slacks fortunately wouldn't be noticeable if she kept her blazer on.

Glancing at her mirror image once more, Brenna checked the gold-studded earrings that graced her earlobes and her makeup. She refused to carry a cache of cosmetics with her, relying on a touch of mascara and eyeliner to enhance her large deep-brown eyes and plum lip gloss accented her full mouth. Satisfied that she looked presentable, she stepped from the car, eager to get a better look at her long-awaited destination.

Judging by the newness of the picturesque tower, bay window, and several chimney stacks, Brenna surmised that the building had been renovated recently. The cream-colored facade, offset by shutters trimmed in a complimentary rust color appeared freshly painted, too. She walked leisurely up the five steps and stopped midway on the porch of the two-story Queen-Anne-styled house. Spider plants and sweeping ivy cascaded from baskets hanging from the porch ceiling. A multicolored porch swing sat off in a corner to the extreme left of the front door. The entire effect was subtle, elegant, and pleasing to the eye. But there was plenty of time to inspect her new home and, taking a deep breath, Brenna knocked on the screen door.

Standing at the door, waiting for someone to answer her knock, Brenna still couldn't believe her good fortune: to be one of two students chosen to work with Jonathan Maxwell was an honor. At least, that was what every other architectural student who applied for the position apparently felt. Brenna, on the other hand, hadn't heard of Jonathan Maxwell prior to receiving belated notice of the contest. The only facts she was aware of were minimal.

He had graduated cum laude from her alma mater seven years ago. Since that time, he had made a name for himself, appearing in several architectural journals. Most of his fame, however, had happened the past year, while she had been abroad. Due to Maxwell's supervision, historic buildings in Philadelphia and Atlanta, ripe with American history had been restored, garnering him accolades from his fellow architects and public thanks from Congress. His restoration of several film celebrities' homes nearly destroyed in a San Bernadino valley fire had also gained him public attention and near-celebrity status. He was now commissioned to restore a Victorian House on Mount Desert Island off the coast of

Maine and Brenna was one of two lucky students chosen as his apprentices.

According to Dean Washington, Brenna's scale-model house plus her high grades were impressive enough to win her this opportunity to work with Maxwell and she had been stunned. It was just what she would have wished for herself—had she thought of it. She didn't want to *teach* architecture; she wanted to apply it, putting her skills and ideas to work. An apprenticeship was perfect.

The door on the other side of the screen squeaked open finally, revealing an elderly gray-haired woman with laughing gray-green eyes.

"May I help you?" she inquired.

"Yes, I'm Brenna Bryant. I believe Mr. Maxwell is expecting me."

"Of course, Ms. Bryant. We've been expecting you alright," she said, in the lilting "down east" dialect Brenna had grown accustomed to the last two days. "My name is Mrs. Winslow. I'm the housekeeper here."

Mrs. Winslow led her to the threshold of a sitting room. "Make yourself comfortable, Miss Bryant. I'll see if I can locate the men."

"*Ms.* Bryant, I assume?"

Brenna thought the voice sounded vaguely familiar, and entering the sun-drenched parlor, she searched for the person behind the voice.

"Michael? Michael Hansen, it's good to see you," she said to the sunbleached blond-haired man who rose from the love seat and grasped her hands.

"Ms. Bryant," he teased again, perfectly impersonating Professor Stanley, the landscape-course instructor who always emphasized *Ms.* when interrogating a female student. "I haven't seen you in ages."

"A year and a half, I think, Michael. Didn't you leave for Greece a few months before I left for France?"

"God! It has been a long time," he agreed.

The two embraced like long-lost friends. In reality, they hadn't been "the best" of friends; rather they did seem to end up in the same classes and eventually developed a good acquaintanceship, based on a mutual respect and fascination with architecture. Nevertheless, Brenna was relieved to find a familiar face.

They swapped anecdotes about their year's study abroad. All was well until Michael asked, "Whatever happened to the fellow who used to pick you up after Stanley's class?"

The corners of her mouth pulled into a frozen smile. A picture flashed in her mind's eye. A picture of her and Clifton Richards huddled at a corner table in the student center. Brenna's eyes darted swiftly to her left hand, her eyes widening imperceptibly at the partial light patch of skin that showed. Deft fingers dove into her straw bag in search of the liquid makeup she had used to hide the evidence of an engagement ring she'd worn faithfully for a year. She realized now that hiding the mark with makeup was juvenile. But she'd been so upset by the termination of her engagement that every time she happened to glance at her naked finger, a feeling of such intense pain would seize her that she genuinely felt she'd never get over the unhappiness remembering brought.

Quickly and coolly she searched her mind for an answer she hoped would satisfy Michael, yet not reveal what had actually transpired between herself and Clifton. Fortunately, she was spared any reply.

The unseen man in the doorway had known one of his assistants was a female but B. Bryant, designer and builder of the Colonial model, wasn't what he had expected. She looked out of place in her chic designer pantsuit. She was probably more at home in gayer, brighter surroundings, he assumed, positive that the backwoods of Maine would not be to her liking.

"So you two know one another. That's good. I'm certain that in the next several months, we'll get to know one another even better. I'm Jonathan Maxwell."

The vision in the formfitting jeans and pale yellow V-neck sweater was a complete surprise. Coal black, tight curly hair—short by today's fashion—glistened in the waning sunlight which poured through the parlor's windows. A pair of sunglasses perched on his nose successfully hid most of his face from view. However, there was no doubting the beauty of his rich brown complexion. This was Jonathan Maxwell?

Michael wasted no time, immediately rising from his seat to shake their employer's hand. "I'm looking forward to working with you this summer, Mr. Maxwell," he said easily, awkwardly grasping Maxwell's extended left hand.

"Nice to meet you, Hansen."

The two men pumped hands; then Maxwell turned to Brenna who still sat, stunned and mute. Removing his sunglasses with his left hand and slipping them into the case in his hip pocket, Jonathan Maxwell revealed the most arresting dark eyes she'd ever seen.

"And you must be B. Bryant. The builder of the Colonial home."

Fathomless eyes surveyed her still-seated form until Brenna finally regained her voice and control of her legs. Rising from the love seat, she seized his hand in what she hoped was a firm grip. She thought Maxwell's insistence that people comply with his awkward handshake was his way of letting it be known that things would be done his way or not at all.

"I'm looking forward to working with you, too," she said, giving him her best leveled gaze, though silently cursing herself for not coming up with something more original to say.

Maxwell's eyes were disconcerting in their unblinking directness. "Yes, I'm definitely looking forward to working with you, too," he replied, releasing her hand. "Would anyone care for a drink before dinner?" he asked, becoming the perfect host.

A wave of relief washed over Brenna when Jonathan Maxwell turned his attention elsewhere. She couldn't believe that she had jumped like a recalcitrant schoolgirl. She was probably more tired from traveling the past two days than she had thought, Brenna rationalized, reclaiming her seat and regaining her composure. Just because her boss for the summer was someone she hadn't expected was no reason to lose the calm exterior she had worked so hard to acquire.

Suddenly a glass of sherry appeared before her. "You didn't say what you preferred. I hope you don't mind my choice," Jonathan stated, waiting for Brenna to take the glass he offered her.

He reminded her of a strong oak tree firmly rooted

in the ground. His nearness and masculinity was so overpowering at that moment that she shrank farther into the love seat.

Jonathan found his new assistant's reaction oddly amusing. Then he chastized himself ruefully. When he learned B. Bryant was a woman, he had determined that her sex did not entitle her to beneficial treatment. She was competent and that was all that mattered. He had to admit that he'd been curious about the builder of the Colonial home; the eye for detail and design was more than he expected from a recent graduate. Well, he had met her so that was that, he told himself, ignoring the fact that when he had first seen her engaged in avid conversation with Michael he thought he had ceased to breathe until Michael moved toward him. He had also noted, he realized wryly, thanks to his 20/20 vision, that except for a thin gold chain around her left wrist and a gold watch, her hands were devoid of any jewelry.

"I guess I didn't hear your offer, Mr. Maxwell," Brenna said graciously.

A trace of amusement touched the corners of his mouth. She had heard him well enough but her musing had gotten the best of her. And they both knew it.

Brenna deftly took the glass from manicured fingertips that grazed her own.

"Chilly?" he queried, solicitously. "Perhaps I should lower the window." Not waiting for an answer he leaned above her, making her all the more aware of the solid expansiveness of his chest and shoulders. In truth, he wasn't a big man, not like a defensive tackle. But at six foot one or thereabouts and one hundred seventy pounds, he carried himself with an easy, confident manner.

"By the way, please call me Jonathan, Brenna," he said, after completing his task. "As I said, we will be working together closely for the next several months."

Mrs. Winslow entered the sitting room and informed the trio that dinner would be served in twenty minutes. "Why don't you all freshen up, especially you, Mr. Jonathan."

"Why Mrs. Winslow, I'm crushed," he responded with a broad smile. "I just washed up," he added, extending his hands good-naturedly for all to see. Which was unfortunate, for on his left hand was a telltale smudge, the color of Brenna's makeup. "Now, where did that come from?" While Jonathan inspected the window he just closed, Brenna retrieved her bags, eager to make a quick exit.

"Can I help you with your bags?" Michael offered.

Good grief. Michael. She had forgotten about him. Had he noticed her exchange with Jonathan Maxwell? Or was she merely making a mountain out of a molehill?

"No thank you, Michael. I can manage. Please finish your drink." From the moment Brenna had learned she'd gotten this job, she was determined to pull her own weight. Besides, if living and traveling in Europe had taught her anything, it was to travel light.

Alone in her room, Brenna placed her small travel bag and large canvas satchel that contained her draftsman's tools on the maple dresser. She mentally replayed all that had transpired since she had entered the boarding house. . . . The exhilaration at seeing Michael, a familiar face; the low of her gauche muteness. A knot on a log would have given a better performance than she. But there certainly wasn't any sense in dwelling over a faux pas that couldn't be rectified now. She simply promised herself that dinner would be a different matter entirely. Her conversation would be witty and informative. She knew how to be charming. She had been in Jonathan Maxwell's company for less than twenty-five minutes but a tenuous tension had seeped through her bones and she knew her employer was at the marrow of it. But Brenna Bryant would be on her toes from now on. Jonathan Maxwell would soon learn that he wasn't dealing with any slouch!

The sun was nearly gone from view by the time Brenna completed her hasty shower and reapplied her makeup. She hurriedly chose a mauve cotton dress with white piping along its mandarin collar and short cap sleeves from her wardrobe, snapping its matching rope belt about her waist. Satisfied with the cool and calm reflection she saw in the mirror, she sprayed on a hint of her favorite cologne, dabbing a few drops behind her ears and on her wrists, which brought the pale band of flesh on her engagement finger to her attention once more. No, she told herself, she wouldn't attempt to cover the patch again. A few days in the sun and she was certain the mark, if not the memories the ring conjured up, would all be behind her. And with that last thought in mind, she hurried to join the others.

At the bottom of the stairs, Brenna turned left and walked across the foyer past the sitting room through the hallway that led into a moderate-size dining room. She paused in the entry way, quickly scanning the room before she was noticed. This was her first true look at any part of the house other than the

outside facade or the sitting room and again she liked
what she saw. The room had an early American fla-
vor, its design distinctly colonial from the creamy
lavender walls to the English furniture that apparently abounded throughout the house. To the left of
the dining table was a fireplace, its logs prepared for
a blazing fire. To the right of the table was a fifteen-
foot-wide china closet filled to its four-tiered capacity
with china, crystal stemware, and a ten-cup silver tea
service. Several paintings of the Maine seacoast and
portraits of early American subjects graced the walls
along with a number of sconces. She could just imagine how the room would look, lit by only a fire in the
hearth and the flickering wall candles. And, at the
center of all this stately luxuriousness was one man—
Jonathan Maxwell.

When she had first entered the room, Jonathan had
been seated at the head of the table, lost in deep
conversation with Michael. Now, however, his eyes
were on her and Michael was nowhere to be seen.

"You look refreshed." He rose from his chair, his
enigmatic deepset dark brown eyes sending a shiver
like an icy arrow through her. How long had he been
watching her, she thought, seating herself on the
chair he held out for her.

"A few minutes ago, you looked as if you were
miles away from here. What were you thinking?" he
probed, in a low, melodious voice. And, feeling he
was genuinely interested, she answered.

"I was trying to imagine what the room would look
like with the fireplace and sconces lit," she replied
truthfully.

His dark eyes held hers briefly. "That can be arranged," he murmured.

Rising from his chair, Jonathan removed the fire screen and adjusted the logs and kindling to his liking. Soon a trace of a flame sprouted, gradually spreading among the logs. Jonathan walked leisurely about the room, dimming the overhead lights while he lit the sconces with a burning ember. Brenna found herself following his movements despite herself.

"I hadn't meant to put you to any trouble . . . uh . . ."

"Jonathan," he supplied for her, turning to hold her with his penetrating stare.

"Jonathan," she repeated, telling herself she might as well capitulate for it wouldn't do to alienate her boss. With tremulous fingers, she swept an annoying coil of hair off her face. Jonathan's dark eyes grew distant and cold, as if her gesture had antagonized him. Why it should she didn't know.

"Excuse me, I've got to wash up again." Brenna wasn't absolutely positive, but she thought his emphasis on "again" was strange. But who was she to judge? And why was she judging him anyway? She *didn't* even know the man. Still, for a few minutes Jonathan Maxwell had disarmed her by his thoughtfulness.

The delicious meal of pot roast, fresh string beans, potato fritters, with mint jelly and hot rolls was eaten in silence. The only conversation had come from Michael and Mrs. Winslow who had both exclaimed how wonderful the room looked, aglow by fire and candlelight.

"Why, we haven't had the room like this in ages,"

Mrs. Winslow beamed. "How nice of you, Mr. Jonathan, to let our guests see the old girl in all her glory."

Jonathan shrugged. What could he say? Certainly not the truth. That seeing Brenna's obvious appreciation of the room had touched him because the dining room was his most favorite room in the house too. Or that once she had voiced her wish he'd immediately envisioned what *she'd* look like in the firelight. Until he noticed the thin pale band on her left hand he hadn't noticed earlier. Until he remembered the brown smudge on his own hand. What little game was Brenna Bryant playing? "Don't thank me. It was the dewy-eyed romantic in Brenna that inspired me to set this mood," he countered.

Inwardly, Brenna bristled at Jonathan's solicitous tone. Dewy-eyed indeed! And to think that she had thought his gesture of lighting the fireplace and sconces had come from genuine kindness, not patronage.

"As you know, Jonathan," she began, placing a little emphasis on his name, "the submission that got me here was a replica of a colonial home. Since I do have a fondness for Early American art and architecture, my desire to see the room in this light had nothing to do with romance."

She nonchalantly passed the bowl of string beans to her protagonist, aware that her comments had hit their mark, judging by Jonathan's errant arched eyebrow. So much for your dewy-eyed romantic, Mr. Maxwell.

"Nevertheless, I still believe you to be a romantic," he continued.

Brenna's eyes darted to the persistent man to her

right. "Oh? Why is that?" she asked laconically, toying with the food on her plate.

"It's just that my first impression of the Colonial model that won you your summer internship was that it had been built by someone in love with the past . . . a romantic, more than likely a woman."

"But why a woman? A man could have turned in a similar project *if* he was as interested in the era as I am," she challenged.

Jonathan seemed to be pondering her last remark. "Perhaps," he chuckled, "but what kind of man?" He cut into the pot roast with brisk, short strokes and popped the morsel into his mouth. Their eyes clashed and Brenna took a sip of her wine. "Actually, Brenna, the miniature furniture was a dead giveaway. You went above and beyond anything I had expected."

Michael eyed the two with unconcealed interest before adding, "Whether Brenna is a romantic or not, I'm glad I had the opportunity to see the room in this light. Whoever designed this room did a sensational job." Brenna agreed.

"Yes, this room is very flexible and versatile, whether three people or ten are dining."

"You two should have seen the place two years ago," Mrs. Winslow said proudly, placing more mint jelly on the table. "Mr. Jonathan did a marvelous job."

Even in the dim light one could see Michael pale while Brenna stifled a gasp. They were casually discussing the merits of the room while the architect himself sat nonchalantly listening to two novices passing judgment on what were probably award-winning designs.

"Well, I'm happy to know you do like the room," Jonathan said, obviously amused, though he at least had the decency not to laugh in their faces. "It *is* quite cozy, isn't it?"

After dinner the threesome retired to the study where a fire was already ablaze in its hearth.

"I love to stay in Ellsworth," Jonathan told them, "but I'm afraid Mrs. Winslow's good cooking puts the weight on."

"Oh, go on with yourself," the older woman clucked as she wheeled in the tea service. Yet she couldn't disguise her delight at the compliment.

Brenna stole a peek at Jonathan who had claimed the large wing chair to the left of the fireplace, his long legs stretched before him. He couldn't be more than thirty-five and there probably wasn't an ounce of fat on him.

"Care to pour, Brenna?"

She wanted to ask him if *his* hands were broken but thought better of it. Where she had stayed in Paris the concierge opened her parlor to her house-guests every Sunday afternoon. Everyone served at one time or another. He'd find no trembling hand here.

It wasn't necessary for Brenna to look up from her task for her to know that Jonathan was staring at her. She could feel his eyes all over her. She gave Michael his cup first, uncaring if bypassing her host was considered bad manners. After all, Michael *was* sitting next to her, she reasoned. The fact that she was fast becoming anxious and irrationally dreaded what she might see in her employer's eyes had nothing to do with her snub. Bracing herself, she raised her eyes and offered him his cup. His eyes, like coal chips, were fastened on her hand. Her left hand. But surely this was all her imagination, for his eyes suddenly lost their intentness and he accepted his cup of tea with a brief nod of his head. Brenna slowly stirred her tea, contemplating the man who had the ability to send icicle slivers down her spine at one moment, before reminding her of their business relationship the next.

"As you know, N. R. Hammond is responsible for our being here," he began.

Jonathan had first met the Chairman of the Board of Hammond Communications three years ago, at a university fund-raiser which was held at Hammond's Washington, D.C., estate. A graduate of the university in the forties, he made his name in the communication field. At last count, he owned seven AM/FM radio stations, two magazines, and a small string of newspapers. But despite his wealth he never forgot those who helped him earlier in his career. He constantly supported his old alma mater financially; the past year the Hammond Communication Center was named in his honor and Jonathan had been the architect.

"In between our periodic professional business—I also redesigned the offices of his flagship station in New York City—I must have conveyed my great fondness for Maine." Brenna noted mentally that Jonathan was possibly from the area. "He vacationed here three years ago and loved the solitude. Two summers ago we revamped this boarding house into a summer place for Hammond and his executives and their families."

However, less than a year ago, Brenna was surprised to learn, Hammond had suffered a mild heart attack. He soon decided it was time for him to turn over most of his empire to other capable hands. Since he enjoyed Maine's solitude and sparse population during his brief vacations, living in the area for at least six months out of the year seemed an ideal tonic for his health.

"Hammond's found the perfect place for his semi-retirement; a large old Victorian house on Mount Desert Island. Unfortunately, the years, few tenants, and the weather haven't been kind to the old girl. That's where the three of us come in," Jonathan stated.

Both apprentices listened carefully to Jonathan's every word. His strong, vibrant voice did not falter once. Although Brenna had been aware of the basic plan of the project, Jonathan made it all sound new and exciting. Nathan Roger Hammond's new home near Seal Harbor was hidden in a grove of resplendent maple and birch trees not far from the Atlantic Ocean. The structure of the house itself was sound, though it was still too small for all of his needs and creature comforts. So it was up to the trio to add rooms and other additions without ruining the line of the building or totally altering the original architectural plan.

"We must work with what there is before us," he emphasized. "Hopefully, we'll be able to match the materials used previously as well. The important point, however, is that the foliage and animal life mustn't be jeopardized," he stated adamantly. "Even if we must eventually provide extra backs and hands, there will be no bulldozers or ball wreckers destroying the landscape or life that exists on Mount Desert Island now."

His intensity held them a moment longer. Both

Brenna and Michael were caught up in the challenge Jonathan presented.

"Any questions?" He looked from one apprentice to the other.

"It appears we have our work cut out for us," Brenna murmured.

"You're not afraid of a little challenge, are you?"

At that moment she would have given anything to know *exactly* what type of challenge he was speaking of. The look in his eyes was puzzling.

"No. A good day's work can be satisfying and this project *is* challenging."

Jonathan cocked an eyebrow and raised his cup in mock salute. "Then here's to a challenging project and a summer of satisfaction."

Brenna looked into her cup before she joined the men in the salute. When she raised her eyelids to steal a glance over her cup's rim, two expressionless dark pools gazed into her own.

The remainder of the evening was their own, Jonathan informed them before he loped off to answer a phone call. Using his absence to slip away, Brenna bid Michael good night. She truly was tired from the day's driving and wished to retire early. Breakfast would be no later than 9:30 A.M., Mrs. Winslow volunteered, wishing Brenna pleasant dreams.

Brenna had just reached her bedroom door, when a sudden urge swept over her. For some reason she was now reluctant to lock herself away in her small but comfortable room. She was probably keyed up by Jonathan . . . Jonathan's speech, she corrected. The fresh Maine night air, she was certain, would calm her and bring the sleep she craved.

Once on the porch, Brenna was glad she had followed the urge. The blue-black velvet sky was sprinkled with stars and a gentle wind caressed the surrounding evergreens and birch trees, making a faint rustling sound in the stillness. She walked to the side of the building, past the porch swing, away from the harsh yellow glare of the front light. The back of the house took on an ethereal appearance bathed only by the light from the moon.

Brenna rubbed her hands up and down the sides of her arms. It had gotten chillier and she wished she had thought to bring a sweater. Surveying the quiet beauty about her, she reached atop her head to unpin her hair, when a shooting star slashed brightly across the sky, then vanished into the darkness.

On impulse, she breathlessly closed her eyes and made a wish, unaware of how provocative she appeared in the moonlight.

"And what do you wish for, Brenna?"

Her eyes sprang open as she snapped around and gazed into the darkness. She hadn't considered someone else would be on the porch, let alone Jonathan.

"Do you make it a practice of scaring your employees out of their wits?" she asked, caustically, even as she attempted to dislodge the barrette from her tangled hair.

"I'm sorry. I didn't intend to startle you," he replied. But Brenna was so flustered she didn't hear the note of concern in his voice.

"Oh, I'm certain you didn't," she responded in exasperation, the tangled barrette sapping her last ounce of patience.

"Surely you don't think I deliberately intended to frighten you?"

"Well, what should I think? You didn't exactly make your presence known, skulking about in the dark," she murmured under her breath.

Unable to release her hair from its confines, she dropped her tired arms to her sides. A resounding laughter rumbled in the darkness and Brenna watched Jonathan's shadowy figure walk into the moonlight. He was actually laughing at her!

"What's so funny?" she asked disbelievingly.

"Skulking is such an old-fashioned word and I'm not certain that it suits you," he chuckled. "You *sound* so belligerent, yet I'm afraid you do look a bit . . . ahh, amusing," he added, indicating the dishevelment atop her head.

She could imagine what she looked like with her hair partially in and partially out of the barrette. Turning away from him, she attempted to yank the offending barrette from her head but only managed to pull out a few hairs by their roots. Brenna felt Jonathan's presence directly behind her and a large, warm hand firmly removed her own.

"I can do this myself," she whispered moving away from his nearness. But he merely pulled her back closer against his chest.

"Oh, I can see that," he muttered, fumbling with the hairclip. "Now don't be silly. Stay still." He turned Brenna around to face him and pushed her head down into his chest as he took a better look at the predicament. In no time he had her hair free and it fell chaotically against her neck. With unconcern he handed the barrette to her and combed his fingers through her hair, fixing it just so. Confused by his gentle touch, she stepped away from him once more. This time he didn't draw her back.

"I really didn't mean to frighten you," he told her. "I usually sit in the back of the house—away from the glaring porch light. It's far more relaxing."

She believed him. Wasn't she herself seeking a hiding place from the harsh luminous glare? And hadn't he stated earlier that he loved coming to Ellsworth and therefore probably stayed at the boarding house often? It seemed only natural that he would have a few favorite haunts about the place. Perhaps she had been hasty with her condemnation, after all.

"I'm sorry for flying off like that. I must be more tired than I thought," she laughed nervously. "I'm sure it was all very innocent." She pivoted to look at him and came face to face with the same expression he bestowed upon her in the dining room earlier in the evening. A shiver zipped through her. He was baffling.

"You're cold." He turned away from her and leaned into the darkness.

"Yes, I am. I think I'll turn in," she murmured. "Good night, Jonathan." And she walked briskly away.

Except for the occasional insect chorus and the rustling of the tree branches, the night was still, yet she barely heard his "Good night, Brenna" over the wind. Had she turned around, she would have seen him gaze after her, an afghan in his arms to protect her from the cold, a look of puzzlement etched on his face.

CHAPTER TWO

When Brenna awoke the next morning, she stepped slowly from the high four-poster bed and raised all the window shades. The sun's rays streamed into the room, making the bed even harder for her to resist. She slithered back between the cool sheets but lay awake, staring out the window and as the cobwebs drifted from her brain two words popped into her mind—Jonathan Maxwell.

The previous evening seemed an eternity ago and the events that had occurred, she was certain, could never happen again, could they? But what *had* happened last night? she asked herself. Nothing, nothing at all. Just a silly misunderstanding. The only other fact of which she was certain was that she had met a man who was definitely . . . different. One moment he was thoughtful, patient; the next, taunting, insufferable, and something else she couldn't quite describe.

She rolled onto her side, shielding her eyes from the glaring sunlight. Good Lord, what was the matter with her? She had come to Maine to work, learn, and recharge her batteries. Nothing more. So why was Jonathan Maxwell getting to her. She sighed deeply, her eyes drinking in her surroundings. One large egg-shape prism splashed rainbow colors across the room. Her gaze followed the dancing lights, down the dresser, across the floor to her hands that lay atop the bedsheet. Instantaneously she knew what was responsible for her erratic behavior: the engagement ring she no longer wore and Clifton Richards.

Clifton Richards. Her college sweetheart, the love of her life and vice versa, or so she once thought when she accepted his engagement ring sixteen months ago. But their impressions of one another had changed with time.

At first Clifton had been an avid listener and talker. Brenna recalled how he punctuated each sentence with his energetic gestures. She found his company enjoyable and, if he showed a tendency for being opinionated, she chose to overlook that flaw. No one was perfect and she felt that, when he offered advice, he always had her best interest at heart. Clifton was a whole new experience for Brenna. She was flattered by his attention and respected his dedication to his career goals. Becoming the second generation lawyer in the family was important to him. She would have staked her life that he respected her dedication to architecture too. But two months before she was to return to the states, a three-month-old torn and dirty college newspaper that finally arrived at her Paris address changed that impression.

One legible page revealed the architecture department's Summer Internship Contest. Clifton had promised to keep her informed of anything that was posted by the department that was pertinent to her career while she was abroad. She had even given him the name of one of her close classmates who had agreed to keep her fiancé abreast of the department's announcements. All Clifton had to do was place the call. So how did such an important opportunity get through the system she had arranged?

The anxiety her fiancé instigated because she had to rush to complete her project was relayed to him in a long, heated letter which elicited no response. Her anxious state never had a chance to subside. Brenna managed to finish her Colonial Home less than seventy-two hours before her flight back to the states. Then there was the packing, the tying up of loose ends at the université, the good-byes, followed by a miserable flight. The opening and repacking of the miniature house for French and United States customs was the final straw on her frazzled nerves.

When she landed at Philadelphia's International Airport, Clifton received a hug and passionless kiss, ten minutes of walking in silence to his car in the parking lot, then a barely controlled tirade of heated accusations once they were seated within the car's closed doors.

Her fiancé had returned her heated words in kind. And it had all come gushing out: his anger at her "avoiding commitment, running after another dream."

"You've seen and done more than most girls from Germantown, Brenna," he stated firmly. "It's time to settle down and make a home. I've got two more years of law school to get through. And, I need your support to do it."

Once he was established, he would see that she had her trips to Europe again and time to indulge her fascination with architecture.

His outburst had come out of the blue. Had he simply tolerated her "fascination" with architecture all this time? No. Clifton had encouraged her to apply for a year of study abroad. She remembered it clearly. How exuberant she felt that she had his support. Later, when she told him she'd been accepted, his response had been less than total enthusiasm. But Brenna had attributed that to the sadness of the reality that they would be apart for at least ten months.

However, she had suggested that Clifton travel with her through Europe before school resumed in the fall. But he had already lined up a summer internship with a prestigious law firm on Wall Street. She had finally succeeded in breaking his sullenness by reminding him coquettishly that the first year of law was hell.

He wouldn't have time for her anyway. She was certain he respected her decision to go abroad, until he interrupted her recollections. "Actually, I never thought you'd be accepted for study abroad, Brenna," he told her brazenly, "I was quite surprised . . . ah, impressed though."

The pain of those words still had the ability to grip Brenna's heart. She forced her eyes open and stared into the bright sunlight, burning away the darkness of her memories.

What she needed to do was address herself to the job before her. She couldn't afford to let this summer assignment and the opportunity it presented slip through her fingers. She'd lost too much already. Clifton. At least the Clifton she thought she had known so well. Yes. She needed to forget Clifton Richards *and* her encounter with Jonathan on the porch last night.

Last night. The memory of her snapping at the man who was her boss for the duration of the summer popped into her mind. Brenna could have cheerfully suffocated herself. "Skulking" indeed, she groaned. He probably thought she was a Class A shrew.

Flinging herself about the bed, her eyes came to rest on her traveling clock. Eight forty-five A.M. No! *Nine* forty-five! Brenna catapulted out of the bed so quickly that the springs screeched in loud protest. Not only would he think her a shrew but a tardy shrew at that.

Although she had dressed in record time, Brenna was still a half-hour late for breakfast. She glanced tentatively into the dining room where Michael sat, reading the newspaper while sipping a cup of coffee, the two neighboring place settings noticeably untouched.

"Good morning." Michael pulled out her chair.

"Oh, don't bother to get up," she replied, curious about his Cheshire Cat smile. "As you can see, I'm running late this morning. I forgot to set my alarm." Her excuse sounded lame to her own ears but it was the truth. She had been so unsettled the night before that she had immediately peeled off her clothes and collapsed onto her bed, not giving her alarm clock the slightest thought.

Stealing a glance at the remaining place setting, she turned her attention to Michael who must have been reading her mind.

"Jonathan received a phone call and asked us not to hold breakfast for him," he said easily, as if he had just supplied the winning numbers for the lottery. "He's a nice guy," Michael added, before returning to his paper.

Brenna chatted, more at ease now that she'd gotten a reprieve from facing Jonathan Maxwell so early in the morning. "You really think so?"

Michael peered around the side of the newspaper. "Oh, sure. I can see why Dean Washington admires him so. And, also why some of your fellow female classmates said they'd give anything to be in your shoes this summer." Smiling sheepishly, he resumed his reading.

Brenna hoped Michael didn't suspect that it was Jonathan, the man, not their employer who had had her off her stride almost from the moment she stepped foot into the house. Just in case, it was definitely time to get his mind moving in another direction.

"I wonder if Mrs. Winslow is still around. Do you think I could get a cup of coffee and orange juice, at least?"

"Oh, sure." Before she could stop him, Michael grasped the small copper bell placed on the corner of the table and shook it.

Inwardly, Brenna cringed, even as the melodious pealing summoned the elder woman.

"Have a good sleep?" Mrs. Winslow beamed. "What would you like? Eggs? Sausage? Pancakes . . . some Canadian bacon? You really should eat something, dear."

"Scrambled eggs and Canadian bacon sounds wonderful, Mrs. Winslow," Brenna replied. "I'm sorry I held you up this morning."

Mrs. Winslow waved her hand airily. "That's all right, dear. Mr. Jonathan said you'd probably sleep late due to the long drive."

So, Jonathan Maxwell had second-guessed her. At least she wouldn't have to look at his smug face while she ate. Still, Brenna couldn't help but wonder if Jonathan actually attributed the long drive alone for her tardiness.

Mrs. Winslow soon returned with a platter filled with scrambled eggs and aromatic bacon.

Brenna hadn't realized how hungry she was. "Hmmmm, smells and looks delicious."

"It certainly does. I see I'm just in time."

No one had heard Jonathan's arrival and, before Brenna could turn in his direction, he had already crossed to his chair and seated himself between his two assistants.

"You really shouldn't have waited for me," he said to no one in particular. "But I'm glad you did. It's more pleasant to eat good food in the company of others who obviously enjoy it too."

Michael, in the process of refilling his plate, was the obvious target of the last comment. But the unembarrassed youth merely smiled and continued to eat with zeal.

"How are you this morning, Brenna? Did you sleep well?" he asked nonchalantly, his eyes riveted to the English muffin he was slathering with butter and grape jam. "You seemed to be a bit under the weather last night."

The cad! If *he* were any gentleman, he wouldn't mention how she appeared last night, at all.

"I was more exhausted from my trip than I realized," she countered, using the excuse he had supplied for her. "You looked as if you could've used a good night in bed yourself."

Fortunately, Michael was engrossed in his newspaper for, judging from Jonathan's startled expression, her unintended barb had hit a soft spot. It was good to see Mr. Maxwell off stride for a change.

"Coffee?" she asked sweetly.

Jonathan nodded, his eyes darting to her hands that poured the steaming brew without spilling a drop. Soft doe-brown eyes collided with luminous dark ones but reflexively turned away, disconcerted by what she saw in his eyes but could not fathom.

During the meal, Jonathan informed them that some of their supplies hadn't reached their working base in Bar Harbor. They would have two or three more days of vacation until the missing material and instruments could be flown in. Since there was now no reason to rush through breakfast, Brenna and Michael settled into a quiet conversation about their travels and Jonathan listened to their tales with interest, barely hiding his surprise when he learned that she had spent some time traveling through Europe alone.

"You don't strike me as a loner," he stated directly. "Weren't you afraid?"

In the very beginning she had had a few homesick moments but Brenna would never admit it to Jonathan. She didn't want him to make any correlations between her handling of that uncharted experience and her present one.

"I would have enjoyed sharing the adventure with my fi . . . a friend," she corrected quickly. Something in the subtle change in Jonathan's features indicating something she said . . . or hadn't said had piqued his interest. "But since that wasn't possible, I went by myself. Don't forget I always had my return plane ticket if things got too hectic for me."

"But you didn't use it," he commented, instinctively knowing once she set her mind to accomplish something she wouldn't falter.

"No, I didn't . . . even though the thought might have crossed my mind once or twice." She laughed at the memory of her apprehension and the two men joined in, lulling her into revealing that, except for college, she had never been far from her Philadelphia home or totally on her own for any length of time.

In many ways, she had grown up in Europe. She had made new friends among her fellow American and French students and had come to trust her own values and judgment. She had contended with many factors and apprehensions plus the language barrier. With obvious pride she confirmed what her sparkling eyes already revealed: she had survived and enjoyed her time abroad with flying colors.

"How did the Europeans react to an American woman traveling alone?" Michael asked. "I found the European women were more than . . . ahhh . . . willing to assist a stranger in their country," he finished innocently, though an impish smile told her Michael's question wasn't so innocent.

From the beaches of Cannes and Saint-Tropez to the sweltering heat of Rome, Brenna had met men of all nationalities, shapes, and sizes. Some had been suave, handsome, and amusing; *all* had been interesting. But she had been able to keep her wits about her and parry their propositions with ease and grace. No matter how persuasive they were, she had kept all at a comfortable distance, a platonic friendship. She had had Clifton, a fiancé. Jonathan watched the display of emotions sweep across Brenna's face.

Finally she said, "I think all men . . . all people

are the same wherever you go. There may be a few extra ingredients to make things interesting—like language or who has the 'home' advantage. But basically, we are all the same."

"I'm glad to hear you say 'we'. For a moment I thought you were going to say that all 'men' are alike." Jonathan gave Michael an unconcealed wink.

Brenna forced a saccharine smile to her lips. She reminded herself that she was here to fulfill a summer internship. She had had new experiences . . . new challenges before. She would not let this new experience *or* Jonathan Maxwell unnerve her.

Leaving the men to another cup of coffee, Brenna opted for a stroll around the house and a breath of fresh, mind-clearing air. She retraced the steps she'd taken around the house the night before. In the daylight it looked so different. Rounding the corner where she had encountered Jonathan, she collided with a second porch swing covered by a glorious, rainbow-colored afghan. Behind the house was a marvelous garden with meticulously trimmed hedges and numerous vined archways, some already sprouting tiny buds, hinting at the beauty of the garden once in full bloom.

"There's stairs down the way a bit," Mrs. Winslow said through the raised kitchen window. "I hope you'll get a chance to see the garden in her full glory," she added as though reading Brenna's thoughts.

She walked down the stairs through the first archway that led into the garden itself. Upon closer inspection, Brenna realized that the garden had been interwoven amidst the vined archways and trimmed hedges. It was a maze! And sequestered away in the nooks of the maze were tiny storybook figures: Thumbelina and Alice's white rabbit clutching his umbrella and watch, the Littlest Mermaid barely visible beneath the small spraying fountain in the center of the goldfish pond were just a few she spied.

At the end of the maze was an old, gnarled stately tree surrounded by a white bench. Brenna took a seat and leaned back against the tree's trunk. She took her sunglasses from the pocket of her khaki-colored jacket when the slam of the back door turned her attention to the house. Jonathan stood on the back porch surveying the garden. Was he looking for her? She put the sunglasses on and studied him covertly as he bounded down the porch steps, heading in her direction. The more he shortened the distance between them, the more aware she became of how he moved, the contours of his broad shoulders, the tautness of his thighs.

"Brenna," he said gingerly, "are you awake?" She nodded and removed her glasses.

"You were so still . . . like one of the statues." He smiled his eyes brightening, his entire face with irresistible charm. "I don't think we have a Sleeping Beauty in the garden. Perhaps you'd like to apply for the position?" he teased.

"The garden is lovely," she responded, and, not knowing quite how to handle his flirtatious comment, she chose to ignore it. "Whoever thought of the statues is to be congratulated. They're a lovely addition."

Jonathan eased himself down next to her; placing his left foot on the bench, he grasped his knee with entwined fingers. "Why, thank you!" he exclaimed. "Two compliments from you in two days, how nice."

Jonathan laughed at her look of obvious amazement. "Don't tell me you designed the garden too?"

"I like to try my hand at all sorts of projects—big or small," he explained. "You should see the garden at night when the fireflies are everywhere and the crickets sound like a small army. It's downright magical, if I do say so. You'd swear you just stepped into a . . ."

He didn't finish his statement, so she completed it for him. "A fairy tale, perhaps?"

His smile was sheepishly endearing. "Yes, that's exactly what I was about to say." He had to be careful with Ms. Bryant. She was a witch who could read his mind.

"And you said that *I* was a romantic," she countered critically.

"Touché, Ms. Bryant. Actually, it was Mrs. Winslow who gave me the idea to add the statues of the storybook characters. She thought the children who stayed at the boarding house would enjoy them and she was right." Jonathan turned toward her and smiled. For once they weren't sparring with one another. It was as if they had mutually declared a truce. The day was bright, the garden peaceful, and Jonathan was so close she could reach out and . . .

"Mr. Jonathannn . . . Ms. Em is on the phone." Jonathan and Brenna visibly started at Mrs. Winslow's interruption.

"Ask her to hold the line one moment please, Mrs. Winslow. I'll be right there."

He turned to Brenna. "I came out here to tell you that Michael is planning a little excursion to some of the neighboring towns. Mrs. Winslow is packing a

lunch. I had hoped to join you two but I see now that
that won't be possible."

The phone call had changed everything. Their
pleasant moment together was gone. So Ms. Em calls
and the great Jonathan Maxwell jumps. Brenna wondered who the woman was. Then deciding to sim-
plify matters she would assume the worse. That Ms.
Em was Jonathan's girl friend. A twinge of disappointment gripped her heart briefly but Brenna
shrugged it off. She shouldn't be surprised, she told
herself. Jonathan was an attractive man. It was only
natural that some woman had set her sights on him.

She slipped her glasses on her face as if to hide her
thoughts from the man who sat next to her, visibly
perplexed by the various expressions that crossed her
face.

"I'm certain Michael and I will have a good time
sightseeing all the same," she said waspishly, even to
her own ears.

Jonathan's eyes widen briefly. Without another
word he loped toward the house, taking the back-
stairs two at a time. Her change in tone baffled him. It
was certainly no way to make points with the boss,
especially if she'd gone to the trouble to hide an
engagement or, worse yet, a marriage as he suspected.

Brenna slumped back against the tree, her eyes
closed to his retreating form.

For the remainder of the day, Brenna worked at
keeping Jonathan Maxwell out of her mind. Fortunately Michael was an excellent and interesting
guide. Having vacationed in Maine on several occa-
sions, he had a good knowledge of the countryside.

Their first stop on the tour was the Parson Fisher House in Blue Hill which was built by the first minister who settled in the town in 1814. Unfortunately, the building wasn't scheduled to open until July 1, a little more than three weeks away. But Michael's tourist enthusiasm prevailed and they were soon on their way to Castine where they visited the Wilson Museum on Perkins Street, not far from the harbor. Brenna was grateful for Michael's company. He didn't mind that she did not have much to say. She assumed he thought that, because the whole experience was new to her, she was in awe of her surroundings and that's the way she left it.

They walked about the museum peering at the exhibits of prehistoric artifacts from various parts of the world, as well as ship models and other local historic items. Michael was impressed by the collection of rocks, minerals, and the numerous nineteenth-century carpenter's tools; Brenna was partial to the kitchen and the Victorian parlor. Unfortunately, the parlor reminded her of the Victorian house awaiting them in Seal Harbor and that, in turn, reminded her of Jonathan Maxwell and why he wasn't with them right now.

Enough is enough, she shouted inside her head. Jonathan Maxwell was an attractive man and, from the little that Michael had revealed about him during their ride, a well-to-do man as well. Gathering from his age and the way his jeans clung to his legs, he was probably a healthy, normal male with all the appetites that went with the label. It's only natural that he had female companionship and, considering the way Jonathan had run off to answer the phone, Ms. Em was probably it.

Of course, there was the other side of the coin. She was—so to speak—on the rebound. Her three-year relationship with Clifton was down the drain. No one likes rejection of any kind and that was precisely what her broken engagement was. A rejection of her commitment, their future. A rejection of her personal goals and dreams too. But that didn't excuse her reaching out to the first available man she met. God, she wasn't that needy.

It was late by the time they returned to Ellsworth but the front porch light beamed a warm welcome and Michael, who had done most of the driving, bid her good night and hurried to bed. Brenna walked gingerly around the side of the house, as she had done the night before. She told herself she wasn't sleepy, that she had every right to take a stroll for a final breath of fresh air. She suddenly stopped in her tracks. What happened to her earlier resolve? Exasperated with herself, Brenna spun on her heels and headed for her room.

The following morning Brenna made certain she was up and about long before nine-thirty. She found Mrs. Winslow in the kitchen, a pot of delicious coffee percolating on the counter.

"I hope you don't mind if I have a cup of coffee in here with you," Brenna said. "The others aren't up yet and I'd prefer not to sit in the dining room alone."

"Oh, I don't mind at all," the elder woman replied good-naturedly, although Brenna sensed something different about the woman this morning.

"Is something wrong?" Brenna asked finally.

Mrs. Winslow hesitated, then said, "I really don't

mean to burden you, dear. But it's my sister," she sighed. "Her doctor and I have been begging her for weeks to have a gallstone operation she desperately needs. So when does she decide to go in and have it done? Today. I got a call 7:30 this morning."

Although Mrs. Winslow appeared annoyed, Brenna sensed the elder woman's genuine concern for her sister's welfare. She knew how trying families could be at times, having older brothers and sisters herself. They could be a nuisance but, at least, let them be healthy nuisances.

"It's too late for me to get my regular help to come in," Mrs. Winslow confided with a sigh, then abruptly straightened her shoulders. "Well, she'll just have to check herself into the hospital on her own. And that will be that."

Brenna sat silently at the kitchen table, not knowing what to say when a bleary-eyed Michael chose that moment to put in an appearance.

"Good morning, Mrs. Winslow . . . Brenna." He said between a stifled yawn. "I see we have the same idea," he said good-naturedly as he took the proffered cup of coffee from Mrs. Winslow's hand.

Brenna motioned Michael aside and whispered the housekeeper's predicament in his ear. After a few moments of conversation they turned to Mrs. Winslow and said, "If you don't mind having strangers in your kitchen, we could fix our own breakfast this morning."

"Oh, I couldn't ask you two to do that," the elder woman replied, obviously touched by their thoughtfulness.

"Why not?" Michael asked. "Don't forget we're recent college graduates. We didn't eat all of our meals in the cafeteria. You have no idea how bland cafeteria food can be."

Seeing Michael's strategy, Brenna quickly joined in. "That's right," she quipped. "I cooked for myself quite often."

Mrs. Winslow looked at Brenna, then Michael, and smiled. "You both are very nice," she murmured happily, untying the apron from around her waist. "But what about Mr. Jonathan?"

"I'm certain if Jonathan knew the circumstances, he'd insist that your sister is more important than our breakfasts," Brenna said firmly, praying she was right in her assumption.

Michael ushered the woman to the kitchen door, offering to take her wherever she needed to go.

"That's all right, dear. You've been more than thoughtful. My old station wagon and I can make it just fine." Before she left, Mrs. Winslow told them where they could find everything they needed. For a moment or two, Michael and Brenna stood in the center of the kitchen and surveyed their surroundings.

"Where should we begin?" Brenna asked finally.

Michael sauntered toward the coffee pot and poured himself another cup. "I think *I'll* have another cup of coffee," he said mischievously. "Where are *you* going to start?"

"Me! You mean *we*, don't you?"

Michael took a seat. "Brenna, I don't know a thing about cooking. You could say I don't even know how to boil water."

"But you *said* . . ." Brenna stammered.

"Yes, yes I know what I said." He leaned back into his chair. "But that was for Mrs. Winslow's benefit. In college I may have bought the groceries, but my girl friend did the cooking."

And, of course, since Brenna was a woman, he had simply assumed she would know all about cooking and love to do it too! "Of all the nerve!" Brenna exclaimed.

Michael obviously knew when to make an exit for he hurried to the kitchen door. "I tell you what. I'll head Jonathan off and let him know our predicament. If you need any moral support, just give a yell."

Brenna muttered a few choice words she was certain would have burned Michael's ears, *if* he had stayed around long enough to hear them. Just because she was the lone female in this little expedition did not mean she would automatically take it upon herself to handle any and all domestic crises that arose. But fixing this morning's breakfast *was* for a good cause, Brenna remembered and she commenced to rummage about in the cabinets and refrigerator until she found everything she needed: settings for three, bread for toast, eggs for the omelets and some cheese to give it a little extra pizzaz, a slab of bacon, and orange juice. That should do it. Taking a black frying pan from its hook on the wall, Brenna placed it on the stove, then tied the housekeeper's bibbed apron about her neck and waist.

"Well, well, well . . . look who we have in the kitchen."

The hairs on the back of Brenna's neck bristled. "Good morning, Jonathan. I trust that Michael has explained the situation this morning."

"Yes he did, but I had to see it to believe it."

Brenna whirled around, ready to do battle but the

look in Jonathan's eyes was warm with no hint of derision to be seen.

"It was really very thoughtful of you to help Mrs. Winslow out like this," he said through sleep-glazed eyes. And he meant it.

"Would you like a cup of coffee?" she offered. "Breakfast won't be ready for a while yet."

Brenna seized the coffee pot, not wanting to see that sleepy look in his eyes or anything else, but it was too late. She had already mentally taken in the blue work shirt he wore open at the neck, its sleeves rolled halfway up his arms. His shirttail hung carelessly outside the jeans Brenna suspected would be his attire for the entire summer.

"I'd love a cup, but don't concern yourself. You have enough to do; I'll get it." Before she could move he reached around her, brushing her shoulder as he grasped the pot. She felt an indescribable undercurrent that she couldn't ignore sweep through her. His cup of coffee in hand, Jonathan leaned against the counter and watched her.

"Well?" *Why was he still here?*

"Well, what?" he replied lazily.

"Does this mean you're volunteering your services?" she asked. Surely he didn't plan to stand there and watch!

"I wouldn't dream of entering your domain," he laughed, thinking she probably couldn't even boil water and preparing himself for the worst meal he'd ever have to eat.

"Since that is the case, I really don't need an audience. Why don't you sit in the dining room with Michael until breakfast is ready?" Brenna suggested, annoyed at the testy tone she heard in her own voice.

"Hmmm . . . a little cranky in the morning, I see. Well, don't get yourself all worked up. I'm leaving," Jonathan replied, obviously enjoying the situation immensely.

"And take the place settings with you," she instructed. "I'm not going to do everything, you know."

Jonathan bowed playfully. "Yes, ma'm."

How could a man be both infuriating and charming at the same time, she wondered.

Although not a gourmet cook by any standard, Brenna congratulated herself on the morning meal. She served three perfectly cooked omelets and hadn't overcooked the bacon either. As they ate, the threesome decided flowers might make Mrs. Winslow's sister's stay in the hospital more bearable. Jonathan volunteered to take care of the arrangements after breakfast.

"May I have another cup of coffee?" Jonathan held out his cup in Brenna's direction and without hesitation she poured.

"Not only can you build a quaint colonial model house but you cook a tasty omelet too. Which of your two talents do you prefer, Brenna," he asked wickedly, "the career side or the domestic one?"

Jonathan watched the display of emotions sweep across Brenna's face with great interest, determined to ask questions until he unraveled her mystery, especially since she hadn't bothered to hide the pale band of flesh since that first day.

"If I hadn't intended to practice my profession, I could've saved myself a fifth year of hard work and study abroad," she said defensively, hearing the echoes of Clifton's tauntings and accusations in Jonathan's words. But she caught herself too late and, floundering, she averted her eyes and reached for the coffee pot, hoping to make light of her response. "Of course, it doesn't hurt to have a second career to fall back on. But a gourmet cook I'm not."

Michael smiled. Jonathan said nothing. And Brenna, too much of a coward to look in a certain direction, tossed her napkin on the table as nonchalantly as possible. "I think I've gotten my domesticity quota for today. So I'll leave the dishes to you two. I believe the dishwashing liquid is under the sink," she said before breezing out the dining room with, at least, *some* aplomb—she hoped.

Brenna paced through the garden, quietly chastizing herself. She would have to learn to consider her every response carefully when Jonathan Maxwell was around. No matter what he said, she mustn't let it faze her. She was here to work, to learn her craft . . .

"Cooled off?"

Lost in contemplation, Brenna hadn't heard Jonathan's approach but her new resolve was firm. "I don't know what you're talking about," she lied.

Jonathan's laughter enveloped the garden. "All right, we'll play this your way. I merely wanted to report that the dishes are washed and stowed away."

"Oh? And did you wash or dry?" she asked, content to continue the conversation in this vein for the time being.

Jonathan gazed at his deep brown hands mockingly, then unexpectedly caressed her cheek. "Does this feel like the end result of dishpan hands?"

His caress soft and gentle, as light as rich angora wool against bare skin, caught her rising humor in her throat. Brenna lowered her lashes to block out his inscrutable gaze and Jonathan pulled away, jamming his hands into his pants pockets. *Now why in the world did I do that?*

"Since the rest of the day is ours," he said a bit huskily, "I thought you'd like to see the pink granite quarries on Deer Isle."

"Isn't that some distance from here?" Brenna asked, vaguely remembering seeing the name on her map.

"Nathan Hammond has placed a helicopter at our disposal in Trenton," he said, surveying the garden. "The trip won't take longer than forty minutes at the most."

"I'd love to see it, then." Brenna smiled. "I just couldn't bear another long car ride."

"Good. I'll see you out front in fifteen minutes." Without another glance in her direction, Jonathan strode away. "By the way, Michael has already seen the granite quarries on one of his previous trips," he tossed over his shoulder. "So it'll be just you and me."

With some trepidation, Brenna awaited Jonathan in front of the boarding house. She had begun to rely on Michael's presence as the perfect buffer between her and Jonathan. This time she'd be on her own and Brenna silently prayed that no faux pas would ruin this outing.

"This isn't quite what you expected, is it?" Jonathan asked, startling Brenna when he pulled up in front of the house in a formidably, rugged-looking blue Jeep.

"I never know what to expect from you," she replied, as she dickered with the camera she decided to bring with her.

"That's funny." Jonathan smiled and shifted into gear. "One could say the same thing about you."

The idea that she was as much a mystery to him as he was to her pleased Brenna. Perhaps he too realized that they had been circling one another cautiously and unnecessarily. Perhaps they had now reached a turning point and the sometimes friendly, sometimes not, attitude would cease.

For a time, they drove in silence while Jonathan guided the Jeep onto State Highway 3 en route to the Trenton airport, shifting the gears with effortless ease. One summer Brenna had attempted to learn to handle a stick shift, but after her first and only nerve-racking, jerky attempt, her older brother had impatiently declared that she was a lost cause and that she'd better pray that automatic transmissions were never replaced. Easing herself into a more comfortable position, Brenna wondered if Jonathan would be a patient teacher.

Brenna stole glances at her companion, as the wind whipped her hair about her face. "Have you always lived in Maine?" she asked, finally breaking the silence.

He turned to her briefly and smiled. "No, but I feel that I have." Brenna's interest piqued. "Actually, I was born and raised in Philadelphia." He opened the glove compartment, removed his sunglasses, and slipped them on. "It's my father's people who are originally from Maine—via Canada and Georgia."

"This sounds complicated," she said, aware for the first time that they were both from the same area of Pennsylvania.

He smiled. "No, not really. My father's ancestors fled from Georgia to Canada through the Underground Railroad. When Lincoln declared the Emancipation, some stayed where they were while others, who couldn't adjust to the different culture, were content with settling in Maine. My grandfather eventually migrated to Philadelphia with one of the wealthy families that summer-vacationed on Bar Harbor. I'm told he hated it here," Jonathan chuckled, leaving Brenna to consider these new revelations. "I was ten or eleven years old when my father first brought us to Maine," he continued.

"And you fell in love with this remote countryside immediately," she surmised.

Jonathan nodded in agreement. "Whenever I visited, my cousins would take me fishing or clamming. Sometimes we'd just go for long walks and talk. Before I knew it, Maine had become a part of me."

Brenna considered what type of boy Jonathan had been. Had he worn thigh-high black boots, like the family she spied wading off the coastline? Was he as unpredictable then as he was now?

"So the grandson of men who relocated to the city has returned to the simple country life-style."

Jonathan chuckled. "Quaint, huh? It got to the point that, even if my parents didn't plan to vacation in Maine, I always insisted they send me here to stay with my grandparents anyway."

He slowed to enter the airport parking lot and Brenna wished the ride were just a little longer.

"I've only been in Maine for a few days, but I can see why you like it so much," she responded quietly. "It can be very peaceful and restful here. Yet the people are so friendly and alive."

"Perhaps you've fallen in love with my Maine too," he said lazily, driving into a parking space.

"Yes . . . perhaps I have," Brenna said quietly, before slipping on her sunglasses and out the car door.

Although Nathan R. Hammond had come to the area barely more than two years ago, his name opened many doors, Brenna learned. She and Jonathan were quickly ushered to the waiting helicopter and in the air in minutes. Brenna had flown in planes many times but this was more exhilarating . . . special. Perhaps it was all due to the close confines of the craft, seated between the pilot and Jonathan whose arm lay along the back of the seat behind her neck. She willed herself to concentrate on her photography.

Jonathan played the role of guide extremely well, pointing out various landmarks of interest as they flew over Mount Desert Island and then the Atlantic Ocean and its ever-threatening waters splashing white foam against the stark, dramatic cliffs. She took nearly a roll of film attempting to capture the water's startling shades of pale gray to aqua-green when it ebbed back to the ocean's depths, and the periodic copses of opulent evergreens that survived atop the cliff's terrain. Brenna was so lost in her camera's lens and the excitement of the moment that she hadn't registered Jonathan's arm about her waist and the fact that she was leaning across his chest in order to see better out the copter's side window. Once this intimacy did register, Brenna reminded herself of her resolve. If Jonathan didn't mind the contact, neither would she.

Not for a moment would she admit that the feel of her shoulder pressed against his chest and his fingertips resting softly on her waist had any effect on her shaky equilibrium when she alighted from the helicopter.

"There are several fireplaces in the Victorian house that were built from this pink granite. Unfortunately, the previous owners didn't keep them in good repair so we'll need to look into that, even though these quarries have been closed for years."

Brenna offered no comment, more absorbed with the sun's rays bouncing off several granite slabs and the roar of the ocean against the cliff. Sea gulls flew above their heads and she wrinkled her nose a few times and breathed in the salty ocean air.

"Excuse me a moment while I speak with the caretaker."

Brenna took several shots of her surroundings, then stood solemnly gazing out toward the horizon. Suddenly Jonathan grabbed her arms and turned her toward him.

"Did you hear anything I said?" A wide smile graced his lips.

"What? Oh . . . you mean about the granite and the fireplaces. Yes, I heard you."

She held her camera in both hands. It was the only thing separating Jonathan and herself. She glanced up at him, but the sun's reflection in his sunglasses prevented her from seeing his eyes.

"Do you usually go away like that?"

"Away?" Puzzled brown eyes looked into his questioningly.

"Yes, I was talking to you but you were far away. For a minute I thought I'd have to do something drastic to get your attention."

Laughing, she queried, "Oh . . . how drastic?"

Taking her words as an invitation, he slowly lowered his head while one hand grasped her waist and the other held the back of her head. Brenna yearned to see the look in his eyes as his mouth grazed her own, working its magic. But the sun's glare prevented it. His lips brushed hers in a light feathery kiss that prickled her charged senses. She had to fight the urge to push her camera aside and wrap her arms about his neck to explore the kiss more fully. Instead, she held her camera tighter and stared into his sunfilled lenses. Then the kiss stopped and he drew away from her.

"I better go speak to the caretaker," was all he said.

She watched him walk away and the tension that had swelled within her swiftly subsided. Why had he done that? What was he trying to prove? Brenna raised the camera and focused on Jonathan standing next to the quarry caretaker. When he looked in her direction, she clicked the shutter several times.

After he finished his discussion, he rejoined her by the cliff's edge.

"Why did you kiss me?" she couldn't help asking him.

"Do I have to have a reason?" Brenna wished he would remove those blasted sunglasses. "I had the urge to kiss you and I did. Surely as independent a woman as yourself can appreciate that, can't you?"

Brenna didn't know what type of answer she expected, but that certainly wasn't it and her confusion must have showed on her face.

"You're such a serious girl," he sighed. "I'm sure I'm not the first man to kiss you."

Jonathan's frankness and flippant reference to her

as a girl irritated Brenna but she was determined not to let him know how disappointed she was.

"Of course I've been kissed," she responded with her own flippancy. "Many times."

"Good, then let's not make a federal case out of this one, shall we?" Jonathan's words stung like salt in an open wound. "Let's just attribute it to a fitting ending to a pleasant day."

"Of course," she said offhandedly, "but just in case another 'pleasant day' comes along, I'll remember to keep my distance." She turned on her heels and walked toward the helicopter. If he put his arm about her shoulder on the return flight, she would remove it, firmly, at once!

The trip back to Trenton was ominously quiet. Jonathan stared out the window while Brenna removed the used roll of film and replaced it with another. Only the pilot attempted any conversation and she tried to show interest. But if Brenna thought the returning flight had been deadly, then the Jeep ride to Ellsworth was even more so. She was so relieved when they pulled in front of the boarding house, Brenna had to consciously control herself from bounding up the stairs. She wouldn't give him the satisfaction of seeing her run inside.

"Hello, dear. Did you have a nice outing?" asked Mrs. Winslow, who greeted their return at the doorway.

"It was pleasant enough but I'm a little tired now." Brenna headed up the stairs for the comfort and seclusion of her room.

"I fixed a late lunch for you and Mr. Jonathan," the older woman said, "and I want to thank you both for the flowers too. My sister loved them."

"I'm glad, Mrs. Winslow," Brenna replied.

Jonathan, who had followed Brenna into the house, stood poised in the study's doorway. He smiled at the housekeeper, the moodiness he had confronted Brenna with during the entire return journey not in evidence now.

"Oh, Mr. Jonathan . . . Ms. Em called," Mrs. Winslow stated.

"Thank you. I'll call her while I have lunch in the study." And he disappeared behind the study's closed doors.

"What about you, Brenna?" she asked.

Brenna continued up the staircase. "Thank you . . . but I'm not hungry now."

CHAPTER THREE

Brenna packed the last of her clothes and placed her few pieces of luggage by the door. She glanced around the room checking that she hadn't left anything behind. Her head still throbbed from a headache that had overcome her in the middle of the night. Perhaps Mrs. Winslow had some aspirin. She would ask her once she got downstairs.

The night before Jonathan had informed his apprentices that they would be leaving for their working base near Bar Harbor. After hearing this news, Brenna had excused herself from the dinner, claiming fatigue from the day's activities. If only that had truly been the case. In reality she had lain in bed wide awake for most of the night, eagerly awaiting the lethargy of sleep. Jonathan's actions at the quarry had left her perplexed and her mind kept replaying the incident until she finally succumbed to exhaustion in the early morning hours.

But today would be different, she told herself firmly. She could see yesterday more clearly now. Jonathan's rebuke of her question had hurt her deeply but at least she had the knowledge of knowing she hadn't responded to his kiss completely, otherwise his dismissal would have wounded even more. Brenna admitted to herself that Jonathan was baffling but she determined not to waste this time—*her* time—figuring out his game. As far as she was now concerned, Ms. Em could have Jonathan Maxwell with her blessing. Her resolve firm, Brenna picked up her luggage and walked down the stairs.

What could have been an awkward breakfast turned out quite pleasant. Brenna had taken her tone from Jonathan's cordial greeting, holding an interesting conversation with her breakfast companions as the men, both of whom had previously been to Mount Desert Island, attempted to prepare her for the sights with a brief background about their summer residence.

"Back in the 1880s and '90s the most socially prominent families of the era—the Morgans, Vanderbilts, Rockefellers, and Fords—made Mount Desert Island, in particular Bar Harbor, their summer retreat," Michael informed her. "If it hadn't been for them, and the elaborate summer cottages they built, we wouldn't be making this trip. Would we, Jonathan?"

Jonathan poured himself more coffee. "Yes, those 'elaborate cottages' were really large and somewhat ostentatious estates that overshadowed much of the rustic charm of the area. Fortunately, the one we'll be working on this summer isn't that pretentious."

"You make it sound as if Bar Harbor were the jet-set port of its day," Brenna offered.

"Actually, that's not a bad analogy," Jonathan said, "for with these new, wealthy families came branches of some of the major stores located in New York and Philadelphia, as well as exclusive clubs which were formed for yachting, tennis, horseback riding, and gala balls."

The young woman frowned. "Is that how Bar Harbor is today?" she asked, not relishing the idea of sacrificing her quiet summer for one filled with a great deal of social hobnobbing.

"No, not really. Though the native Mount Desert Islanders feel Bar Harbor gets spoiled by the summer vacationers, most times I find it relatively quiet and respectable. I believe one of the Rockefellers still has a hideaway in the area. You see, in 1947 a disastrous fire destroyed many of the cottages and the island was never quite the same." Jonathan looked at her quizzically. "Don't you like the idea of spending the summer rubbing shoulders, more or less, with the rich and famous?"

"I value my privacy as much as anyone, Jonathan," she responded, surprised she could speak his name without feeling a dull throb of sorrow in her chest, "and my commitment to this summer's undertaking is as important to me as their life of leisure is to them. I'm looking forward to the work but more importantly, the solitude."

"You'll find Bar Harbor a beautiful, neat town that slopes down to deep-water anchorage." Jonathan surveyed her briefly before finishing his coffee. He wondered just how committed to the project she was. How true was her little speech?

He wondered if her lips were as soft today as they were yesterday. He downed his coffee to the dregs and placed his napkin on the table. "Everyone ready to go?"

Brenna left her car in Ellsworth to be picked up later and traveled in the Jeep with Jonathan and Michael who entertained her with tales of the Abnaki/Wabenaki Indians, the "people of the dawn," a once-powerful nation of more than twenty tribes that inhabited parts of Canada, Maine, New Hampshire, and northern Massachusetts. As Brenna listened to their stories, she watched the scenery change from the occasional resort hotels and motels that lined the major freeway to Mount Desert Island, through the town of Bar Harbor itself, to its outskirts where seaside aster, black-eyed Susan, sweet clover, pine, birch, and oak trees abounded. She marveled at the diverse terrain she had seen in this one state— from the rolling farmland, to the forests and rugged mountains, to its vast wilderness areas and rugged seacoasts. Somehow it seemed right that Jonathan would love this state so dearly. He was so much like it in his own way. As the Maine countryside continued to surprise her with its uniqueness and changeability, so did Jonathan. The previous night of turmoil and unhappiness was forgotten. At breakfast he had treated her with a cordiality which she had returned. And now, in the close confines of his Jeep, his veneer slipped more and more until the three talked easily like long-lost acquaintances instead of employer and employees. Perhaps he had been right; she shouldn't make something out of an innocent kiss.

"Here we are," Jonathan said finally as the tree-lined roadway opened to a clearing.

Before them stood a two-story house of wood and glass with a veranda surrounding the second level. It blended perfectly with the grove of pine and birch trees that encompassed it.

"It's beautiful," Brenna exclaimed walking across the short wood bridge that led to the main entrance, glancing briefly at the stream below.

Brenna was so involved with the house before her,

she didn't notice Jonathan's eyes skipping along her supple curves, taking in her every movement. She didn't see his mouth curve into a quizzical smile as he pondered the look of perplexity on her face. "Something wrong?" He stopped halfway up the path to the front door.

"There's something about this house that's familiar."

"Perhaps it's the design?"

Brenna cast a critical eye over the house once more, then smiled slowly. "You've taken the design for a mill and updated it, haven't you?"

His rich buoyant laughter echoed through the trees. "Can't fool you, can I?" Jonathan resumed walking up the path, with Michael a close second, and Brenna a very slow third. By the time she reached the door, Jonathan had already ushered Michael inside and stood smiling in the doorway.

"Didn't you find memorizing all those architectural facts and designs boring?" He reached for her tote bag and placed it on the table by the phone. His question was unexpected and she hesitated for a moment before speaking.

"I . . . I never thought of it as boring . . . hard work, yes, but never boring." Brenna returned his glance expecting him to say something further. But Jonathan waved her in the direction that Michael had taken, without uttering another word.

The inside of the house was more fabulous than its outside facade. The living room was richly decorated in warm orange and umber tones. A brown velvet sofa was placed strategically in front of a large fireplace which looked as if it had been used often, while on the opposite side of the room stood a spiral staircase. Michael had already placed his suitcases down and was casually browsing through the extensive record collection on the east wall.

"This place is fabulous," Michael murmured as he inspected the elaborate stereo system. While the two men swapped stereo know-how, Brenna contemplated the living room from the elegant African sculpture to the brightly colored collage-like paintings of Romeare Bearden. All the artwork was chosen with care and she suspected they were all originals, not copies. She couldn't see Jonathan accepting second best in anything. She turned to the men once more but her eyes were only interested in Jonathan and she committed to memory the broad width of his shoulders molded snuggly in a khaki and blue cotton tee shirt that tapered into fitted jeans. Brenna had been around attractive men before, men who shared her love of architecture too, yet she could not pinpoint her peculiar response to her employer. Not wanting to be caught staring at him, she walked to the floor-to-ceiling curtains on the west wall and pulled them back, exposing a breathtaking view of the stream not more than ten feet from where she stood.

"Like it?"

Brenna looked up at one of the two men she would be sharing this house with for the rest of the summer.

"Hmm . . . yes, Jonathan, it's lovely." Her voice sounded disturbingly husky even to her own ears.

"Want to see the rest of the house?" She nodded, eager to see her room—her home away from home until summer ended.

Placing the last of her clothes in the armoire next to the brass bed, Brenna opened the sliding doors and stepped out onto the veranda, walking the short distance to the railing. She looked back at her room and smiled. Her guest room was decidedly aimed toward the female gender. A pale coral downy-soft spread with matching dust ruffle and pillow cases graced a dazzling brass bed, a hope chest at the foot. A walnut armoire, makeup table, and porcelain jug, and wash basin balanced out the room nicely.

She marveled at Jonathan's good taste but what she liked most about the room wasn't the furniture but the wall behind the head of the bed. Photographs, some of which were dated as far back as the 1890s, added the final historical touch to the room. It was a contrast to the more modern living room but if Brenna had to choose which room she liked the most she'd be hard-pressed to decide.

A cool breeze blew from the west and Brenna deeply inhaled the fresh air. The view from the veranda was breathtaking. On one side of the house she saw acres of timber and a widening stream. Walking to the back of the house, she was pleasantly surprised to find a patio and a tree-lined path which appeared to wind through the dense thicket. The faint sound of the pounding surf in the distance and the tangy ocean scent in the air caused her to wonder what it would be like to live in this setting all year round, to watch the trees' leaves change color in the fall, see the onslaught of snow, the stream frozen over, and spring's first thaw.

Continuing her walk around the house, she passed what she presumed to be Michael's room, judging by the suitcases, and then reached another set of sliding doors and what had to be the master bedroom. It was at least twice the size of the other bedrooms and had a huge king-size platform bed which dominated the room. Across from the bed was a fireplace. For a brief second a picture of Jonathan asleep in the huge bed with a blaze in the fireplace settled in her mind. Brenna chided herself for thinking of her employer in that manner and quickly completed her tour of the upper floor before seeking out the men below.

She found them at the opposite end of the house from the living room and kitchen, setting up draftsman's tables, filing cabinets, and other materials they would need for the summer. Brenna began to sort the original blueprints and floor plans from some preliminary scale drawings Jonathan must have done, along with other, as yet unmarked and unlabeled, papers. She could see that it would take a few days to get everything properly marked and filed away.

"How are you coming along?"

Brenna glanced up from her work and smiled hesitantly at the man who towered above her, his tee shirt hanging outside his pants and a fine film of perspiration glistening on the rich brown skin at the base of his throat and across the bridge of his nose. "I think it will take me a while to sort all this."

Jonathan nodded, then stopped and absently leafed through the reams and reams of paper. "I'm afraid the previous owner of these blueprints didn't take good care of them. But among the three of us we should be able to place them in proper order."

Michael looked up from his task and smiled in agreement.

"Yes, I think we'll make a good team," Jonathan said.

They worked in companionable silence for most of the afternoon until Jonathan noticed that several boxes of office supplies were missing. He glanced at his order form and double-checked the number of boxes with those they had opened. Finally he folded the paper and stuffed it into the back pocket of his jeans.

"Everything isn't here." There was no doubting the annoyance in his tone as he walked across to the picture window. "Perhaps some of the boxes are still at the post office," he thought aloud. "I think I'll drive into town and check into it."

"Do you mind if I come along?" Michael asked. "I've got some letters to mail and I would like to pick up a few postcards."

"Sure, I'll meet you at the Jeep," Jonathan responded, then turned to Brenna. "And what about you? Care to come along for the ride?"

Part of Brenna didn't want to lose the feeling of camaraderie that had been growing among the three but she also wanted some time to herself.

"I'd like to stay here," she replied. "I want to look around a bit."

"You're certain you'll be all right?" Concern flickered briefly across his face.

"Certainly, unless there are bears out there," she said gesturing toward the forest that surrounded them, "waiting to pounce on the first edible thing that passes."

Jonathan's laugh was warm and reassuring. "You might spot a few deer but that's about it," he said. His laughter glowed in his eyes. "We shouldn't be gone long."

The remainder of the afternoon Brenna spent wandering about the grounds. She spotted a doe sipping at the stream's edge and followed it along the gurgling water upstream for a while. However, after a time she retraced her steps and took the path behind the patio. The route toward the ocean was closed in on either side by trees and dense undergrowth, but, as she drew closer to the sound of the waves pounding against the shoreline, the trees began to thin until she found herself looking out on a stretch of land strewn with small rocks, pebbles, shells, and several boulders. She walked a little distance, perched herself on one of the boulders, and glanced out in the distance. She spied a few sailboats but nothing else. She was totally alone. At first she thought she would walk down the beach to the point where a towering cliff jutted skyward. But it was getting chillier. The sun had started its descent so she changed her mind. There would be other days to explore the coastline. She had the entire summer before her.

Exhilarated, Brenna returned to the house only to find that Jonathan and Michael had not yet returned. Tired from her afternoon excursion, she decided to take a soothing bath and then nap until the men returned. Gathering her toiletries from her dresser, she went through the doorway Jonathan indicated led to one of the two bathrooms in his home. When she flipped on the bathroom light she gasped in delight. A raised platform held a sunken tub that was easily big enough for two adults. The room was decorated in greens and browns with several potted plants and overhanging ferns giving it an outdoors feeling. Behind the tub was a floor-to-ceiling curtain and, when she pulled it back, she received a view of the stream winding off into the forest.

Enchanted, Brenna turned on the hot water and threw in the scented bath tablets she located next to the tub. Quickly removing her clothes, she walked up onto the platform, then eased herself down into the tub. Looking about the room more carefully now, she startled herself when she caught her reflection in the mirror opposite the tub. Was that how she really looked? She had piled her hair atop her head and her brown skin glistened with the perspiration from the hot water, her shoulders and the beginning swells of her breasts barely visible. She wondered how Jonathan would react if he saw her in this setting. Temporarily caught up in her musings, Brenna saw the room more clearly from her vantage point, noticing the two adjoining wash basins. Closing her eyes, she sank deeper into the hot soap-bubbled water. This had to be the master bathroom and she tried not to wonder with whom Jonathan had shared this luxury.

Completing her bath and drying herself with one of the plush bath sheets she found in the linen closet, Brenna went to her room and fell asleep.

Sometime during her sleep it began to drizzle and she awoke to darkness and a coldness that permeated her body. She turned on her bedside lamp and donned her warm fleece caftan. Surely Jonathan and Michael had returned. Yet as she crept down the stairs, only darkness greeted her. Where were they? Had they encountered some problems? Certainly

Jonathan could manipulate the roadway to his own home even with the rain and the darkness.

Chiding herself for her panicked thoughts, she walked into the living room, groping for the table lamp she had seen earlier. A warm yellow light soon bathed the room and she tried to start a fire in the hearth but failed miserably. She couldn't even locate the thermostat to raise the temperature. Now thoroughly disgusted, Brenna decided she would have to settle for a warming cup of coffee or tea. But first she'd put some music on the stereo to drown out the stillness. Perusing Jonathan's collection, she found he had a wide range of records including jazz, classical, and country western, to her surprise. A new release from Wynton Marsalis caught her eye and she placed it on the stereo.

Accomplishing this one task, the soothing melodious trumpet filled the emptiness as she walked down the brief hallway that led to the kitchen. It was raining harder, she noted, as she rummaged through the cabinets. She had just located a container of hot chocolate when the kitchen's back door flew open and a soaked Jonathan walked in.

Both of them were caught off guard by the other but Brenna reacted first, dropping the can while lurching back into the kitchen counter. Her eyes were wide with fright.

"My God, I'm sorry, Brenna," he murmured as he stripped off his windbreaker. "I seem to have a knack for frightening you."

Jonathan placed his wet jacket on a peg behind the door. Brenna shivered noticeably before he realized he hadn't shut the door. "Not only have I frightened you but now I'm going to give you pneumonia, too."

Her laughter caught shakily in her throat. "Oh well, I was fixing myself some hot chocolate anyway. It's rather cold in the house and I couldn't find the thermostat to turn up the heat."

"I see that when I showed you and Michael the house I neglected a few things," he muttered. "Why don't you fix me a cup too and I'll see if I can raise some heat. Ok?"

Nodding her head, she poured milk and hot chocolate in a pan and placed it on a burner. She had just finished pouring the hot liquid into two mugs when Jonathan returned.

"It gets quite chilly along the coast even at the height of summer," he cautioned. "Add to that the rain and our nearness to the ocean and the result can be lethal."

Brenna picked up her mug. "All ready," she mumbled, acutely aware of how Jonathan's wet sweater and jeans clung to his body, emphasizing his masculinity.

Jonathan grabbed his mug and ushered her into the living room where a glowing fire blazed in the hearth.

"I suppose you attempted to start a fire," he teased congenially.

"I'm afraid my secret is out," she shrugged languidly. "I flunked campfire building as a Girl Scout." Brenna seated herself on the sofa in front of the fire. Jonathan left the room briefly, returning with a quilt that he tucked about her waist and legs.

Surprised, Brenna barely heard herself utter, "Thank you."

"You're welcome."

The two sipped their drinks quietly with Jonathan

occasionally leaning closer to the fire in an attempt to dry his hair. The strains of the music grew stronger and stronger but instead of relaxing Brenna they grated on her uneasy nerves. *His* presence and the knowledge that they were alone made her feel awkward.

"Where's Michael?"

Jonathan looked up at her from his place on the rug. "He's in Ellsworth."

The stunned look on her face, although fleeting, did not pass unseen by the man sprawled before her and he explained.

"The post office forwarded some packages to Ellsworth, since that was where the call to locate the first missing materials originated." He took another sip of his chocolate. "Michael hitched a ride with a friend of mine. He'll pick up the missing parcels and drive your car here."

Jonathan surveyed the young woman closely as she removed a piece of lint from the quilt. "I think I'll make myself more presentable," he said. "Would you like more to drink?"

"Yes . . . if it isn't any trouble." Anything to get him out of the room for a moment.

Before Jonathan went to change, he returned with a pot of hot chocolate and a plate of cookies.

"My great aunt always sends me a care package of these things," he offered with a boyish smile, then left the room.

Brenna bit into one cookie. Oatmeal and it was delicious. She poured herself more chocolate and eased back into the sofa. Never in her wildest imaginings had she thought she would be alone like this with Jonathan. Well, it would be short-lived, she thought, because Michael would be back soon, she was certain. As she ordered her overimaginative mind to cease its fevered wonderings, Brenna helped herself to another cookie, not hearing the faint ringing of a telephone above the music.

Jonathan soon returned dressed in black sweat pants and workshirt and resumed his lounging position before her. He helped himself to a cookie, eating it in two bites. In the firelight his dark eyes, reflecting the orange flames, never strayed off her face. Thinking how vulnerable she was and how little she knew of the man seated before her, she shuddered.

"Are you still cold?"

Brenna took a hasty gulp of her chocolate and shook her head no. Yet he still reached out and effortlessly lifted her, quilt and all, onto the shaggy rug next to him.

"I said I wasn't cold," she murmured in weak protest.

"If you're not cold, then why the shiver?"

Damn the man!

"It's nothing," she said, feeling like a butterfly half in and half out of its cocoon, for she was now hopelessly tangled in the quilt. Why did he have to speak so softly? Why did he have to show her how thoughtful and gentle he could be? Why couldn't he just eat his damn cookies and drink the chocolate without asking any probing questions?

"What are you afraid of, Brenna?"

And he had to be perceptive too. Brenna sighed, "Nothing, what's there to be afraid of?"

The fire's flames danced to the stirring last refrain of the trumpet's slow ballad. Eerie shadows pranced about the room while Brenna avoided the urge to look into Jonathan's eyes.

"Perhaps you're afraid of me," he said matter-of-factly. Taking another sip from his mug, his eyes were still locked onto her face.

Brenna knew it wasn't Jonathan as much as herself that she was afraid of but, affronted by his conceit, a biting retort formed on her lips. However, when she looked into his face, his deep-set eyes were her undoing for in their depths she saw something ominous . . . something smoldering.

With the ease of a cobra who, having hypnotized its prey, lashes out suddenly, Jonathan took their mugs and placed them on the table.

"Perhaps to be more precise, you're afraid of this."

In the back of her mind Brenna had entertained the idea that this very thing could happen but the possibility of its occurring was nothing compared to the reality of his embrace. The warmth of the fire was a poor substitute for the heated waves that swept through her as he gently yet persistently nibbled her full mouth. With a curious detachment they gazed into each other's eyes, fencing to see who would break the moment first. Gradually Brenna became aware of his hands moving up and down her back, massaging her tension away. His feathery light kisses heightened the volatileness of their situation and she shut her eyes, shivering slightly.

A muffled groan escaped his throat and their veils of aloofness slipped away. Jonathan gently opened her mouth with his lips and she gave herself up to his touch, returning his passionate embrace in kind. He enjoyed the warm haven he found once he parted her lips and Brenna was astonished at how swiftly he had swept her away into this new, heady experience. He continued his entreaty slowly, tickling her mouth's inner softness, then retreating to lightly brush her lips with the tip of his tongue only to invade her delicate mouth once more.

Her hands stopped caressing his back, to wander along his side to his firm chest. The workshirt he now wore had come partly unbuttoned, and her fingers tentatively touched his nakedness for the first time. "Yes . . . touch me," he murmured in a jagged breath.

Spurred on, she deftly unfastened the remaining buttons, then guided her arms around him once more. Hesitantly she stroked his muscular back with her palms and fingernails and he shuddered against her. Moving his mouth languorously across hers, he pressed her pliant form into the rug. Her senses reeled from the clean fresh smell of his still partially damp hair and the rhythmic pelting of the rain on the house. It seemed he couldn't get close enough to her but she needed air and, as if sensing her need, he removed his lips from hers only to commence a new assault on her ear with his tongue before kissing a burning trail from her earlobe to the base of her throat. His new overtures fanned the flames of her desire. She knew if he wanted to possess her she wouldn't stop him. Then suddenly his movements ceased and he merely held her tightly in his arms. His warm ragged breath gently caressed her throat. With passion-glazed eyes he looked down at her. For the first time Brenna was self-conscious by the fact that she lay prone beneath him.

"Don't ever be afraid of me," he commanded. His desire was etched across his face, his look so intense she couldn't find her voice, so she nodded mutely her acquiescence.

"No matter what does or doesn't happen between us, I hope we'll always be friends."

She closed her eyes, certain her desire was as evident to him as his was to her. Eyes shut, she felt his lips brush hers and, without hesitation, she parted them. His touch was soft, gentle, and fleeting.

"You seem to be tangled up here," he said easily as he moved from her and saw the bind she was in. "You weren't able to get away from me, were you?"

His teasing banter eased her embarrassment as he released her from her binds. Brenna felt awkward lying on the floor while Jonathan walked around to flip the record over and turn off the lone lamp. She also felt confused. There was no denying the fact he was her boss, for heaven's sake, and she had broken her own cardinal rule about getting involved with any superior, be he professor or employer. Still what had happened between her and Jonathan came about so naturally. So right.

"Cookie?"

She laughed and ate the cookie that he dangled before her. Jonathan laughed too, nuzzling her neck from behind as he fit the long length of his body against hers. Brenna surrendered to his nearness, relishing the weight of his hand splayed possessively atop her stomach. It was then that Brenna remembered she had nothing on under her caftan. Feeling her tense, Jonathan kissed her cheek and whispered, "Remember your promise."

She wasn't afraid of him, she told herself. But as the flames danced before her, lulling her to sleep, she pondered the gnawing sensation in the pit of her stomach.

Turning in her sleep, Brenna raised her hand to remove the heavy weight from her hip, only to grasp a warm hand. Shocked awake, she found the room almost in total darkness except for a few glowing embers in the fireplace. Suddenly she recalled everything and her heart palpitated rapidly as she attempted to remove herself from her place on the floor. She was thankful that the room was dark for she soon realized that her robe had crept up around her thighs and strong male legs tangled about them. Cautiously, she eased herself from his embrace when one strong hand grasped her hip tenderly and pulled her back.

"You're awake, I see." Jonathan's husky voice broke the stillness.

"Yes . . . ah . . . have you been awake long?"

In the darkness he leaned over her, searching for her lips with his fingertips. Finding them, he placed several kisses on her mouth.

"I *was* sound asleep until you tried to leave me."

Brenna could barely ascertain his face in the darkness so she was left to wonder if he was teasing her or not.

"It's late," she murmured, attempting to pull down her robe as nonchalantly as possible. Understanding her intentions, Jonathan chuckled. He untwined his limbs from hers, then helped lower her gown, his knuckles grazing her thighs as he did so.

"Feel better now?"

"Yes . . . but I should go upstairs . . ." A finger halted her sentence, replaced by firm male lips. When he released her, she tried to speak again.

"But Jonathan . . . what about Michael?" Brenna flinched. Had Michael already returned, found them in their compromising situation and gone on to bed? She was mortified at the thought.

"Don't worry about Hansen," Jonathan said. "He called while I was changing. He'll be spending the night in Ellsworth and will rejoin us in the morning."

He had known Michael would not be returning.

"Why didn't you tell me this earlier?" she asked.

"I didn't think it was important," he said, oblivious to her changing tone.

His unconcern for her feelings was like dousing a cat with cold water. Clifton and his maddening ways streaked into her mind. He had also taken her feelings for granted and to see Jonathan repeat the same scenario dampened the entire evening.

"You didn't think it was important?" She noticed the pulsing vein in his taut jaw. The eyes she thought warm and loving only a few minutes ago hardened. He sighed, exasperated. "Why . . . would it have made a difference?"

Anger swelled within her as Brenna scrambled to a sitting position. Just *how* naturally had what transpired between them come about after all, she seethed. "You knew Michael wouldn't be back tonight. You planned this whole seduction," she accused.

He cursed silently and moved away from her. The table lamp suddenly came on.

"May I remind you that you were in your flimsy robe when I returned home and that you already had the music playing seductively." He flung himself on the sofa, his annoyance clearly etched on his face.

"But you took full advantage of an innocent situation," she retorted.

Jonathan leaned swiftly toward her, causing Brenna to jump from her position on the floor.

"You can't tell me that you didn't want or enjoy what happened," he said harshly. "I think it's a bit late for the hurt, innocent act." With a sickening feeling Brenna rose from the floor, leaving the quilt in a heap at her feet.

"I don't have to stay here and listen to your conceit," she muttered.

His contemptuous laugh startled her.

"Did you say conceit or *deceit*, Ms. Bryant?"

Brenna looked at him but his eyes revealed nothing.

"What are you raving about?"

"Cut it, Brenna. Just cut it. Exactly what are you protesting?" Jonathan's lips twitched, a snide expression altering his appearance, "the fact that we were making love and could have been interrupted? Or are you angry with yourself about this and trying to assuage your guilt?" He grasped the third finger of her left hand.

"Did you conveniently remove the ring the minute before I met you at the boarding house?" he asked roughly. "I bet you have the little gem upstairs in your room and chastely put it on your finger every evening before you retire."

A wave of nausea threatened to overwhelm Brenna where she stood. She looked at her finger. Yes, it was obvious that she had worn a ring recently. But that was over and had been behind her ever since she dropped the diamond in Clifton's mailbox before she left the university. Jonathan had her all wrong but she wouldn't grovel; she wouldn't explain anything to him.

"So you don't deny that you have an engagement ring?"

She looked at him directly and managed to say coolly, "My affairs are of no concern to you."

"An appropriate choice of words," he replied sardonically. "Go to bed, Brenna."

He strode to the fireplace, grasping the mantle with his hands. Brenna raced up the stairs, slamming her bedroom door behind her. How could he think she could make love to one man while engaged to another? How dare he think that of her? *He* had manipulated the evening, not she. An impotent rage seized her body and suddenly she felt cold and alone and far from home.

CHAPTER FOUR

The sounds from the awakening forest and the dawning day could not eliminate the memory of the preceding night. Brenna woke from her dreamless sleep, her robe rumpled about her, the coverlet clenched tightly in one hand and haphazardly wrapped about her.

Rising, he opened the curtains a fraction and returned to her bed, propping herself up against the brass headboard with a pillow. What a mess! A summer that had looked so promising only a few days earlier lay shattered before her. After last night's performance she was positive Jonathan Maxwell would be handing her her walking papers. Brenna fabricated different excuses he could give Michael—and Dean Washington for that matter—upon her removal from the project. Incompatibility? Artistic temperament? Or a blunt "it just wasn't working out."

Her eyes strayed to her left hand and a pitiful excuse for laughter seeped through her lips. Jonathan was so damn observant, too observant for his—and her—own good.

She recalled the day in May a little more than a year before when Clifton Richards had asked her to marry him and given her an engagement ring. She had worn the gem the entire time she was abroad.

She remembered how effectively its sparkling presence had discouraged even the most brash would-be European suitor. Unfortunately, last night the ghost of the ring chose to exert its presence once more, successfully driving a wedge between herself and Jonathan—on *any* level permanently, she suspected.

Brenna jumped from her bed and marched to the shower. When had he said he first noticed the pale band of flesh on her finger? From the moment she first arrived? But it hadn't bothered him until she denied him what he wanted. The ironic fact was that Brenna knew last night she wouldn't have denied Jonathan anything—*if* he hadn't been so devious and manipulative.

She shampooed her hair and lathered her body with soap and silently told herself she would not give up her summer without a fight. She knew that, if she succeeded, Jonathan could make her summer one long tortuous hell but it would be worth it. Despite what she thought of him personally, she knew she could learn a great deal from Jonathan. The experience and his name on her résumé with a description of their summer project could make a difference when she looked for employment, a difference in her career. And, above all, she did want to be an architect. Jonathan Maxwell wouldn't send her packing without a great deal of difficulty and she was determined to give him plenty, if she was forced to.

Downstairs the grandfather clock in the hallway chimed the half hour. She rinsed herself, quickly dried off, and rummaged in the hope chest for fresh lingerie. Brenna opted to wear her navy short-sleeved khaki pantsuit with a red- and white-striped tee shirt. She looked nautical as she resolutely walked down the stairs to seek out her employer. She marched to the work area but, although she saw several new packages—obviously Michael had returned —no one was about. Hearing the clatter of pots and pans, she stealthily walked to the kitchen.

"Good morning. I'm Mrs. Newland, Mr. Maxwell's part-time housekeeper."

Brenna returned the woman's greeting, somewhat relieved not to have come across Jonathan so quickly.

"If you're looking for Mr. M. and Michael, they're on the patio eating breakfast. Waffles and sausage all right for you too?" she questioned.

"Yes, that sounds terrific."

Stiffening her backbone, Brenna tried to control her nervousness as she mentally told herself to give one general greeting to both men and take her seat. Taking a few calming gulps of air, she opened the back door and walked around to the patio.

"Good morning."

"Good morning, Brenna." Michael rose from his seat. "Glorious morning, isn't it? Smell that sea air."

Jonathan didn't even glance in her direction but when Michael rose to seat her he cavalierly got to his feet too and his smile was mocking when he asked, "Sleep well, I trust?" Obviously not expecting an answer, Jonathan picked up his folder and leafed through the contents. At least the battle wouldn't begin until after breakfast, she surmised, when Michael wasn't present.

"Did you see much of the area yesterday?" Michael asked, genuinely interested.

"I followed the stream upriver for a while. It gets wider as you go along. There's a well-worn path right along the bank." Brenna's face came beautifully alive as she shared her walk with Michael. "I saw several small animals in the underbrush but they moved so fast I couldn't quite make them out. But I did see a beautiful fawn on the opposite bank. Next time I'll have to remember to take my camera. I might get some interesting nature shots."

Mrs. Newland arrived with a tray of waffles with strawberry preserves, bacon, orange juice, and coffee and placed them before Brenna.

"This smells divine, Mrs. Newland." Her mouth nearly watered at the sight of breakfast and without hesitation she dove into the pile of waffles. She wouldn't give Jonathan the satisfaction of thinking her appetite had waned because of last night's events.

"There's plenty more if you want it," the house-keeper said, picking up an empty tray as she reen-tered the house.

"What kinds of animals did you say were in these woods?" Michael asked, picking up the conversation where they had left it.

"I only recognized the fawn." Then she added hesitantly, "There aren't any dangerous animals near here, are there?"

Jonathan put down his folder and answered as a matter of course. "You needn't worry. You probably ran into some squirrels or chipmunks. Besides the deer, you're likely to see beavers, muskrat, maybe a weasel, or a fox."

"No bears?"

"Black bears are rare visitors to the area." Jona-than's lips formed an odd little smirk. "Don't worry. We'll try to see that you don't get eaten by one dur-ing your stay."

So, she *would* be staying on the island for the duration of the project.

Jonathan resumed his perusal of his notes and she watched him while she ate. His piercing dark eyes were lost in thought as he wrote down note after note. Tiny lines showed at the sides of his eyes and corners of his mouth when he frowned, making him look older and more foreboding. In his casual white terry sport shirt, his muscular brown arms rippled. There was no denying the virility of the man sitting opposite her and with a sigh Brenna turned away. At least she still had her summer job. She shouldn't be greedy; she couldn't expect everything. Last night probably saved her from any future encounters with her boss. A total business relationship was really the best.

Although his outward appearance was calm and indifferent, the previous night's occurrences had been on Jonathan's mind too. At first he had been so angry, he considered firing her on the spot. But the project hadn't begun yet. And he couldn't think of any simple explanation that would justify Brenna Bryant's dismissal. Worse yet, although he was angry about last night's turn of events and *still* hadn't figured out his apprentice's games, Jonathan ruefully had to admit that he was still inexplicably drawn to Brenna. It was unfortunate that he didn't trust her. Regardless, she had signed on for a summer's work and he was determined that she'd definitely earn her keep. This was one summer he'd make certain she'd never, ever forget.

"I want to take you both to meet Mr. Hammond this morning," Jonathan said, breaking the silence. "It's only a thirty-five minute ride to the house he's renting outside of Seal Harbor. As soon as you're finished eating we can get started."

Jonathan unfolded his linear frame from his chair and headed for the kitchen. Where was the angry, brutally frank man she had seen the night before? Had he chalked last night up to "one of those things"? Or was he merely biding his time. Brenna didn't like this cat and mouse game but, for the time being, there was nothing she could do. He would have to make the first move and, keeping that thought in mind, she attacked another waffle.

The trip to Nathan Hammond's vacation home went quickly. In Jonathan's Jeep they maneuvered the backwoods roads with relative ease and were soon pulling up in front of a lowlying structure. Although the Hammond house had plenty of wood and glass like Jonathan's, this house was more contemporary in design, lacking any rustic charm. However, there was no denying that in its own right the house was spectacular.

"He's out on the sundeck, Mr. Maxwell." Godwin, a somber manservant with a lilting island accent, had answered the door, recognizing Jonathan immediately.

"Thank you Godwin, no need to show us the way."

Brenna and Michael followed close behind Jonathan who strode confidently through the house, through the salon to the sliding doors that led to a teak wood sun deck.

"Jonathan, good to see you." Nathan Hammond embraced Jonathan warmly. For some reason Brenna hadn't expected this sign of affection between the two men.

Nathan Hammond cut a jaunty picture in his blue

sportshirt, white pants, and deck shoes. He was a good two heads shorter than Jonathan, but what he lacked in height he more than made up for in his bearing. He wore his salt-and-pepper hair cut very close and his warm brown eyes sparkled merrily from a dark brown weather worn face.

"Nathan, I'd like you to meet my two workhorses for your project," Jonathan continued. "Brenna Bryant and Michael Hansen."

Jonathan stood aside while Hammond looked the two young people over.

Hammond shook Michael's hand and gallantly kissed Brenna's fingertips.

"Jonathan, you couldn't possibly turn this lovely creature into a workhorse," he said in mock horror. "That would be a waste."

"Perhaps I should find something else for Brenna, if a workhorse isn't to your liking, Nathan." Brenna refused to acknowledge Jonathan's comment, concentrating instead on the gregarious Nathan Hammond who was leading her to one of the deck chairs.

"Is this your first trip to Maine, Brenna? You don't mind my being so informal?" he asked, ringing an old ship's bell that was attached to a corner of the patio table.

"No, of course not," Brenna demurred. "And to answer your question, this is my first trip to Maine."

Godwin soon advanced on the foursome with a tray of refreshments, and Michael and Brenna told Mr. Hammond of their visit to Blue Hill, and Castine and Brenna relived her two-day adventure driving up the Maine coast. Jonathan seemed content to sit back and let his apprentices do most of the talking, only occasionally offering a comment of his own.

"It seems to me, Jonathan, that you have chosen two excellent people to work with this summer." Jonathan inclined his head in agreement. "I'm so glad that you both love this land as I do. Perhaps you have an idea why I want to live here at least six months out of the year. You should see this area in the fall and during the first snow of winter." The old man sighed contentedly. "But I will need a place bigger than this. More guest rooms and other conveniences."

The apprentices looked about them. You couldn't exactly call Nathan's present residence small. From the teak deck that stretched the length of the house, they could look out over the Atlantic Ocean from their perch three hundred feet above the rocky coastline.

"Do you think you'll have any difficulty making my September deadline, Jonathan?" A look of concern clouded Hammond's face.

"No, Nathan. Now don't worry. The blueprints for your new home plus a replica of the house will be ready in time for your party in the fall. We'll have all winter to work on the interiors." Jonathan spoke reassuringly, the way one would speak to a concerned child about missing a birthday party.

Brenna had known that Nathan planned a huge party with his family, friends, and business colleagues in attendance when he made the announcement of his retirement to his beloved Maine.

"I know I shouldn't worry, Jonathan—especially if you're in charge. You'll overtax yourself getting it done, if I know you." Hammond glanced at Jonathan pointedly.

"Let me worry about me," Jonathan rolled his eyes

heavenward and laughed. "Worse than a mother hen, this man."

The familiarity between the two older men was a pleasant surprise. It was obvious they respected and cared for each other.

"Since we're out this way, Nathan, I thought we might drive over to the house so these two can see what they'll be remodeling."

"Good idea, Jonathan. I'll just zip into the house and speak to Godwin. Excuse me."

Nathan Hammond's dream house was an 1880s' wonder complete with a paddle-wheel motif in the lower railing which had one time circled the entire house. Hammond beguiled his guests with a story of the house's previous owner, a seafaring captain who made a fortune importing and exporting goods and built the home for his young bride. Part of the house had been damaged in a storm and had been rebuilt but the original design had not been followed. Now it was up to Jonathan and his colleagues to rebuild the house accurately.

Michael checked the inside of the house and Brenna walked around the outside, envisioning how the Victorian house would look once all the work was done. This would be another feather in Jonathan's cap. She would not be surprised at all if several of the architectural journals decided to do a spread on the renovations.

"You seem lost in thought, my dear." Nathan's approach across the unkempt lawn hadn't been detected. She turned, expecting Jonathan to be with him, but the other man was nowhere in sight.

"I was just thinking how beautiful your new home

will be once we've had a chance to work on the new plans," she said honestly.

"Yes, I'm sure Jonathan will do his very best, and judging by what he's told me of your credentials, you're a valuable asset."

Brenna looked at the man quizzically. "Excuse me for prying, Mr. Hammond . . ."

"Oh, call me Nathan, please. It'll do my ego good to have a beautiful young woman like yourself call me by my first name. Otherwise . . ." he chuckled, "I'll feel ancient."

She laughed. She was going to like this man.

"Well . . . Nathan, when I was offered this position by Dean Washington, I was under the impression that *you* had hired me. I thought you knew all about me."

The old man smiled sheepishly. "I hope you're not disappointed but I didn't have anything to do with hiring you directly." He lifted the girl's hand, casually tucking it into the crook of his arm as they walked about the grounds. "I only supplied two things for this project—the house itself and the financial backing to get the job done. It was Jonathan's idea to pick two competent students from our old alma mater."

"Oh . . . I didn't realize . . ."

"Oh, yes, Jonathan's quite a man. He's never forgotten where he's come from." Hammond's voice was filled with admiration for his chief architect. "When I first met Jonathan, he was in his third year of college and I had just provided a few scholarships. Jonathan was one of the recipients. I met him with the other winners at a university fundraiser and was immediately impressed with his vitality and his ideas. I knew even then that he would go far."

The two walked completely around the grounds, stopping on the gravel driveway in front of the house.

"I followed his career closely and was able to help him find a position with a firm in New York City," Hammond explained with a smile. "They had a time keeping the reins on him for his three-year apprenticeship. Jonathan was far ahead of his employers in design and innovation. After he became a certified architect, he branched out on his own and the rest—as they say—is history."

The old man looked wistful and a smile creased his mouth. Brenna looked at him for a second, then spoke hastily, "You love him, don't you?" Now why had she said that! How presumptuous of her to meddle and ask such a personal question.

"He's like the son I never had, my dear." Nathan squeezed her hand warmly and led her up the stairs of the house. "You are a very observant young woman, Brenna, and I'm glad you're a part of this project. I hope you'll consider me a friend."

Rounding up Jonathan and Michael, the foursome returned to Nathan's home. At his insistence they stayed for lunch and were treated to a succulent meal of fresh lobster. Having seen the house, the project came to life for them and both apprentices had hundreds of questions and ideas. By the time the meal was over, a bond had developed among them all and they were eager for the actual work to begin.

On the return trip to Bar Harbor, Brenna stole glances in Jonathan's direction. The Jonathan Nathan had revealed to her sounded kind and considerate, saving his ruthlessness for his work to accomplish his various projects on time. She simply couldn't reconcile the man she had seen the night before with the one Nathan Hammond helped her to see today.

When they arrived back at Jonathan's home, he informed them that their work would begin in earnest the following day.

"I saw you walking with Nathan earlier." Jonathan's eyes narrowed slightly. "What were you talking about?"

"Why . . . why the house, of course . . . the project."

"Good . . . just keep it that way," he ordered. "I don't want Nathan to get hurt, while you look for someone to play second fiddle to your main beau."

He turned on his heel and headed back to the Jeep. For a brief second Brenna was stunned. Surely, he wasn't implying what she thought he was!

"Let's get one thing clear, Mr. Maxwell," she said through clenched teeth. "I'm here to do a job and nothing more. Mr. Hammond is a nice man. I like and respect him but I already have a father. Do we understand one another?"

"Perfectly."

"Good!"

Brenna bounded onto the bridge, her heavy footfalls conveying her anger. He watched her storm off with her long-legged strides, her indignation so genuine that, for the first time, Jonathan considered he may have misjudged her altogether.

When her alarm went off at seven-thirty, Brenna felt as if she'd just closed her eyes. Breakfast wasn't served until nine but she wasn't taking any chance of being late. Her position was tenuous enough as it was. The night before, she couldn't stop herself from reevaluating the past two days and the more she thought about them, the more her emotions churned from embarrassment to confusion, then anger. Around and around, over and over, until she'd finally concluded it was futile and masochistic to rehash what couldn't be changed. What *was* important, she finally rationalized, was that she had salvaged her summer internship. She had gotten a second chance and this time she planned to do everything by "the book." And that meant getting down to breakfast on time, but after a long, hot, invigorating, and fortifying shower to bolster her newly found spirits.

Jonathan was noticeably absent when Mrs. Newland served breakfast that morning. By ten o'clock Brenna and Michael had retreated to their work area where the clutter of draftsman's tables, director chairs, desk, and a half-dozen unopened boxes and packages of various lengths and sizes was in startling contrast to the calm, orderly world visible through the picture windows.

"Do you suppose we'll have any room to move around in?" Michael asked, stepping carefully around each obstacle.

"I know what you mean." Brenna opened up one of the director chairs and sat down. "Just unpacking everything and getting organized looks like an awesome task."

"Well . . . since Jonathan's obviously running late, why don't we show a little initiative," Michael suggested. "We have to begin somewhere."

Brenna and Michael worked well together. They set up the tables, attaching portable overhead lamps, and were just about to tackle the boxes when the crunching sound of tires on gravel announced Jonathan's return. Brenna took a few calming breaths . . . By the book she repeated.

"You can leave this stuff for tomorrow," Jonathan said, entering the room. "I've got other plans for you two today." He cleared off a corner of the desk and sat down, unaware how his jeans delineated his muscled thigh.

"I've done a dozen or so quick preliminary sketches of the house from different angles and at different times of the day," he explained. "Now I need to define the ideas in those sketches. That's where you and your camera come in, Brenna." His face was an expressionless mask. He was looking right through her she was certain. "I'll need a panoramic view of the building and the adjoining landscape. Think you can handle it?"

Jonathan held several rolls of film in the palm of his hand.

"Yes, I think I can," Brenna answered confidently, taking the film.

"As for you, Michael, I've got something a little more strenuous in mind." He turned to face his other apprentice. "We'll need up-to-date sketches of the property lines, roads, new utility locations, trees . . . there's a man-made pond somewhere that's not on any geographical layout. Who knows what else. You up to it?"

An accurate portrait of the site could possibly influence the final shape of the house. Michael's task was as formidable as Brenna's and could take more than one day.

"Sure, no problem, Jonathan," Michael replied, swallowing his Adam's apple.

"Good. I had Mrs. Newland pack you lunch." Jonathan rose off the desk. "You think you can find your way to the mansion from here, Michael?"

"Yes."

"Okay. Guess I'll see you two later at dinner. We eat at six."

Brenna collected her camera, tripod, and Michael's sketch pads and pencils while Michael saw to the lunch hamper and checked the Nissan for the trip.

"Dean Washington *did* say we'd be *work*ing," Michael said sliding behind the steering wheel at her request.

"Yes he did. But somehow I'm getting the feeling that he understated this case," Brenna quipped.

Seeing Nathan Hammond's home-to-be the second time around was as exciting—and intimidating—as the first and for a moment the two apprentices stood rooted staring at the formidable four-bedroom, ten-room mansion with half a dozen pink granite fireplaces and other peculiarities only a sea captain could dream up.

Michael moved first finally. "It's 11:30 now. Let's meet back at the car at one for lunch. Okay?"

Brenna agreed, then picked up her camera and tripod, wondering how Michael would begin surveying ten acres of land. She hoped the one geographical layout they had was helpful even though it was sixty years old. But Brenna had her own concerns and, loading the color film, she mounted her Nikon on the tripod and lined up her first shot.

At one o'clock Brenna had completed shooting the

mansion's exterior, taking two or three pictures of each angle. She'd have plenty of time to photograph the surrounding landscape.

"Don't tell me you're finished already!"

Brenna looked up in time to see Michael step out from the grove of trees that sheltered the back of the house from the bitter north wind. "Half way," she smiled. "Hungry?"

"Hot! Can't you tell?" Michael followed Brenna to the car and eagerly accepted the cup of iced tea.

"You do look a bit done in." Brenna gestured at the handkerchief headband he wore and his disheveled appearance.

"Yeah. And I'm only a third of the way finished. Still, it's not as bad as I thought. The mansion takes up most of the land. Let's sit over there." He snatched up the picnic basket and Brenna grabbed her father's old army blanket she kept in the trunk of her car.

"My neck's going to be stiff tonight. I know it."

"How many pictures have you taken?" He handed her half a pastrami on rye.

"Too many. Two-and-a-half rolls," she admitted.

"And you've only done the house?" he asked incredulously. "What did you do? Take a picture of *every* nook and cranny?"

"Don't laugh at me, Michael." She tried not to laugh too. "Jonathan's got me so . . . nervous."

"Oh? I thought you two . . . uh, we all," he corrected, "were getting along just fine."

"Yes we were . . . are. Oh, I don't know, Michael," she said in exasperation. "This job means a great deal to me. I just don't want to blow it. You know."

"Yeah, I know. It's not like we'll be able to take an incomplete if we aren't doing well." Michael reached for another sandwich. "A good recommendation from Jonathan Maxwell couldn't hurt an unknown architectural graduate looking for a job in the *real* world." His smile was infectious. "More tea?"

Brenna held out her cup, thankful that Michael was there for the duration of the summer too.

"I propose a toast—to the *real* world," Brenna tapped her cup against his.

"To the real world," Michael repeated. "Ready or not . . . here we come!"

The sun was an orange ball of startling beauty, setting behind the mountains when Brenna pulled up beside Jonathan's Jeep.

"At least we'll have time to take a quick shower." Michael climbed stiffly out of the car.

"You're reading my mind," groaned Brenna who could practically feel the hot pulsating spray on her neck and shoulders.

The duo made it to their respective rooms without encountering Jonathan in their bedraggled condition but a hasty shower, they both agreed later seated in the small dining area off the living room, couldn't soothe all their various aches and pains.

"Are you as hungry as I am?" Michael sipped the last of his peach schnapps and licked his lips.

"Famished. It must be the hard work and fresh air." Brenna pushed up the sleeves of her black cotton jumpsuit, enjoying the rustic ambiance that surrounded them.

Jonathan rolled their dinner in on a two-tiered cart. "Dinner is pretty informal here," he said, himself ironically dressed in a black crewneck sweater that made him look devilishly disarming until their eyes met and it seemed as if he were looking right through her. "Mrs. Newland prepares our meals during the week," he continued. "We're on our own for the weekend, but she usually prepares several casseroles or preseasoned roasts in the freezer." He swept the covers off their Cornish hen and wild-rice dinner and placed them on the bottom tier of the cart. "All we have to do is follow the instructions she attaches for the microwave."

The small round dining table made it impossible for Brenna to avoid sitting next to her nemesis.

"So. How did things go today?" Jonathan asked finally taking his seat. "Michael?"

"I'm about two-thirds finished." Jonathan nodded. "The terrain was easy to travel through the large copse of trees that shield the house from the easterly winds. But, once you head inland, past the pond there's a rocky incline. Steeper than the chart indicated."

"Sixty years of rough Maine winter weather can do that. I'm surprised you got as far as you did." Jonathan passed the rolls and butter to Brenna without a glance. "I wanted you to survey the land first on foot to get a real feel for the place, the way Nathan will see it when he lives there. But tomorrow you can finish your sketches from a helicopter. I'm sure you'll find it easier on the legs." Michael smiled appreciatively, then dove into his meal with relish.

"And how far did you get, Brenna?" Brenna quickly swallowed her mouthful of food. "I'm finished."

"The entire house and surrounding landscape?" Jonathan queried.

"Yes."

"Did you get a good shot of the driveway, from the main road leading up to the house?" Jonathan poured a dollop of white wine in his glass and tasted it. At that moment Brenna hated everything about her employer, including his superior attitude and endless questions.

"I took pictures of everything, Jonathan. The house and surrounding landscape. Everything. Five rolls' worth of film," she informed him, barely concealing the testiness in her voice.

"I'll have the film developed tomorrow. Wine?" he offered graciously.

Brenna eyed him warily. "Yes . . . thank you."

"We'll see how many shots we can use then," he added, turning to fill Michael's glass.

He's got some nerve, Brenna fumed. She would have to be totally inept not to have gotten one good shot of every angle as he requested and he knew it. But why should she expect better from Jonathan Maxwell? Didn't he think she was an unscrupulous tease? Wasn't their truce on shaky ground as it was? Better she keep the reins on her temper and not expect a pat on the back or a job well-done from him.

After dinner Jonathan showed his apprentices how to use the dishwasher, then retreated to his work area with the rolls of film and sketches while Brenna and Michael settled down to a game of backgammon.

"I'm sorry, Michael, but we'll have to play another time." Brenna rotated her neck in a circular motion slowly. "I can't bear to look down at the board for another minute."

"No problem." Michael rose from his chair. "How about some TV while I try to work those kinks out." Michael slid back the cabinet doors in the wall-to-wall unit revealing a twenty-five inch portable TV that Jonathan had hooked up to a communications satellite disc which was located halfway up the side of the mountain.

"Thanks, Michael." Brenna closed the backgammon set. "You're a lifesaver."

The sketches Michael did were good, very good, Jonathan decided, comparing the sketches he had done a few months earlier to those of his apprentices. But he shouldn't have been surprised; Michael had learned his craft from the same faculty and alma mater as he. Jonathan stubbed out his cigarette and grabbed up all the sketches. At least Michael knew his stuff, Jonathan amended, turning off the lamp attached to his draftsman table. Brenna Bryant was another matter.

Jonathan expected to find his apprentices huddled over his backgammon set so he was unprepared for the scene he walked in on. Brenna was seated in front of his TV with Michael perched on a bar stool behind her, vigorously massaging her neck. What the devil was this woman up to now, he wondered. Her eyes were closed, her lips curved into a beguiling smile. She was obviously enjoying her massage and surprisingly that irritated Jonathan more than he cared to admit.

"Your additions and corrections are really fine, Michael," Jonathan said, making his presence known.

"Thank you, Jonathan." Michael took his sketches. Brenna didn't need to turn around to know that

Jonathan stood directly behind her now. "Something wrong, Brenna?"

"Just a stiff neck from bending over a camera tripod," she said lightly.

"Well, tomorrow there'll be more of the same. While Mike's flying the friendly skies in a helicopter, you and I have to finish putting your work area together."

"Oh I'll be ready," Brenna said firmly, retrieving the tube of Ben-Gay from her pocket. "You needn't worry. I'll be able to handle my share of the work."

Tuesday morning and Michael's departure came too quickly for Brenna who dawdled over a final cup of coffee for as long as she possibly could. But all the anguish she subjected herself to—the tossing and turning the night before, the heart palpitations and now four cups of coffee that felt like churning acid in the pit of her stomach—was laughable for all the attention Jonathan paid her. At precisely ten o'clock he descended from his loft work area like a god descending from Mount Olympus, barking out one command after another for two solid hours until the apprentices' work area, supplies, and blueprints were put in their proper places. His impersonal attitude toward her angered Brenna at first, then fueled her energy as she worked silently beside her taskmaster until Mrs. Newland announced lunch.

"Would you fix a tray for me, Mrs. Newland? I'll be working through lunch," Jonathan informed his housekeeper. "Michael should return around two. As soon as you finish lunch, Brenna, I want you to label all the blueprints clearly. Separate the originals from the renovation blueprints," he ordered, "and do be careful with them. Some are fairly brittle."

The fiery gleam in Brenna's eyes did not escape Jonathan and he grudgingly admitted she had carried her own quite well, working quickly and efficiently for two hours. But two days weren't an entire summer, he conceded, climbing up the loft stairs two at a time.

Jonathan's indifference hurt Brenna, that she could not deny. *But you won't intimidate me off this project, Jonathan Maxwell,* she vowed. *So don't even try.*

CHAPTER FIVE

Brenna poured herself another cup of coffee from her thermos as she flipped through the last pages of the magazine she was reading. Leaning against the incline that led from the patio and short outcropping of lawn to the stream below, she stared at the rippling, crystal-clear water. Another Saturday. Her fourth Saturday in Bar Harbor. A month had passed, yet Brenna felt she had been there much longer. It was the work. Never had she lost herself in her work as she had with the Victorian house. From ten to five P.M.—if they were lucky—she and Michael worked and worked. Jonathan was a relentless taskmaster, checking and rechecking measurements, studying the original blueprints as well as any plans that were made for subsequent remodeling. It had taken them four weeks just to get the basic concept of the house, the *parti*, on paper for Jonathan had brooded about extending the driveway behind the house and the effect it would have on the terrain.

Putting down her cup, Brenna raised her arms behind her head and stretched languorously. It was unseasonably warm, about 83 degrees, and a white-yellow sun brightened the day, forcing her to hide behind her sunglasses. For two weeks Jonathan had his apprentices working all hours—through their lunch breaks, sometimes into the dinner hour. And on Saturday it wasn't unusual for him to request that they drive to "the house" to double-check measurements. If it hadn't been for Nathan, who had arrived unannounced one Saturday and found her up to her elbows in blueprints, Brenna might be at her draftsman's table even now, instead of lounging in the early afternoon sun.

Brenna smiled at the recollection of Nathan's chiding Jonathan for his zealousness before firmly stating he didn't want Brenna or Michael to work all the time. He wanted them to enjoy their summer too, hence they should not work on Saturday or Sunday. Jonathan had been a little taken aback by Hammond's adamancy but yielded, although grudgingly, to the older man's will.

A splash from the far side of the stream roused Brenna from her thoughts. Sitting confidently on a rock was a bullfrog. She watched him as he hopped about surveying his domain, then vanished into the undergrowth. If there was one thing she would never get enough of, it was the barren beauty of nature around her. Sometimes when she and Michael went for walks—Jonathan rarely joined them—they would find patches of flowers in the forest—golden heather, pink lady's slipper and wild iris. Frogs, squirrels, chipmunks, and deer abounded as well and some of the smaller, more adventuresome creatures had gotten so used to their presence that they'd come up to the breakfast table for a few crumbs, much to her delight.

Yes, thank heaven for Saturday and Sunday, she thought. Her time was her own. Today she would drive into Bar Harbor or Ellsworth and stock up on a few more magazines or paperback novels. Yet, although she was glad for her free time, it was those nonworking hours in the evenings, Monday through Friday, which were the hardest to get through. Sometimes she and Michael would play backgammon or Scrabble in the evening but more often than not Jonathan and Michael would be lost in a chess match. At those times her only recourse was to bury herself in a book or, if she were lucky, there might be a good program on TV.

She was envious of the easy rapport between the two men. Both Jonathan and Michael were gracious losers—although the elder man won more than he lost—and the chess games forged another bond between the men. Their chess matches were closely fought and many a night Brenna watched Jonathan squinting through a cloud of cigarette smoke, a small snifter of brandy nearby, as he contemplated his next move. Then, when the game was resolved, she watched them joke good-naturedly and recap the one fatal move that had decided the outcome.

Yet except for work and passing out instructions, Jonathan hadn't had much to say to her since they began working in earnest. The first two weeks had been unbearable, she recollected. Jonathan had constantly criticized her handling of the blueprints and the accuracy of her figures. If it weren't for the fact that Dean Washington had told her specifically that the accuracy and care for detail in her model home were the factors that had clinched for her her present position, Brenna couldn't say she would not have packed her bags long ago.

Brenna picked up her magazine and thermos bottle and walked up the slope to the patio. If she was going to go into town, she had better get started. Her thermos rinsed thoroughly, she hurried to her room for her purse and a jacket, just in case it cooled off while she was gone. She walked through the living room, stopping at the telephone; there was a message, written by Michael. It read simply: "Jonathan, call Em." Brenna turned away swiftly and headed for the spiral staircase. Since that night four weeks ago, Jonathan had not touched her again. The relief Brenna expected by his indifference didn't materialize. And the idea that he had easily relegated their encounter to one of unimportance angered her.

Shaking her head ruefully, she picked up her sweater and hurried to the kitchen to raid the refrigerator. A few pears to munch on sounded good to her. Stooping over, she retrieved two pieces of fruit, which she placed in a brown paper bag. When she turned around, her eyes encountered Jonathan lounging against the back-door jamb. He didn't speak, just openly surveyed her from her slim ankles up her gracefully trimmed legs to her casual shorts. She had not seen that blatant look in his dark velvet eyes since her first night in his home and a funny warm feeling began to grow in the pit of her stomach. She had to get out of the room.

"Excuse me," her voice faltered, "but I was just on my way out."

"Yes, I know. That's what I've come to see you about," he said throatily. "I lent Michael the Jeep. His girl friend is visiting this weekend and he needed transportation. Michael said you were going to Ellsworth and I'd like to hitch a ride."

She had told Michael she would be going to Ellsworth *or* Bar Harbor, but wouldn't be surprised if

Jonathan had deliberately stated Ellsworth because that was where *he* wanted to go.

"I had planned to shop in Bar Harbor," she said boldly. "I don't think I'm up to driving to Ellsworth."

Jonathan opened the back door and escorted her out into the sunlight. "That's no problem. I'll drive," he stated succinctly. Brenna bristled at his authoritative tone. She contemplated an equally succinct retort when Jonathan spun around and said softly, "I really would appreciate the lift, Brenna. It's important."

She hadn't heard that husky tone in his voice for a long time. For a second she held his gaze, then flipped him her car keys.

He backed the car smoothly down the driveway, knowing his plea of lack of transportation was just a ruse. One phone call to Nathan and he would have a car. But for the last two weeks he had watched Brenna work and she was good. Michael and she got along extremely well too. And now he was having second thoughts. Maybe he had misjudged her. Maybe she hadn't been trying to hide anything from him after all? Or at least had a good explanation for his suspicions. All he did know was that the more he was around her, the more he wanted to be with her. The more he wanted to know about her.

The sun reflected off Jonathan's sunglasses as he drove the Nissan through the busy town of Bar Harbor onto the road that led to Mount Desert Narrows, the only way other than by boat to get on and off the island. The silence in the car was painfully noticeable and Brenna turned on the radio.

"We don't seem to have a great deal to say, do we?" he commented, glancing briefly to catch her eye.

"No . . . no we don't . . . but we shouldn't feel that we have to. We can just share this wonderful day," she responded.

"Yes, it is beautiful. You should get out more often, see the sights. Have you been to Somes Sound or the Thunder Hole?"

"Well, actually I haven't. This is only my second free weekend," she said innocently.

Jonathan's lips curved into a luminous grin. "I walked into that one, didn't I? When Nathan gave me that tongue-lashing, I almost expected him to box my ears. Was I really such an ogre?"

She tried to be as diplomatic as possible. "Let's just say you had your moments."

He laughed again, then winced. "That bad, huh?" Brenna laughed too, feeling as if a great weight had been lifted from her shoulders. Or was it her heart?

For the next twenty minutes Jonathan beguiled her with more tales about the history of Mount Desert Island. She learned about the Plymouth Pilgrims who had halfheartedly claimed the island and established temporary fur-trading posts but found the area too remote and rugged and too near the neighboring French strongholds. She was surprised that the founder of the Hudson River School of painting, Thomas Cole, had migrated to the area to find, as Jonathan aptly put it, "something new to paint." After a time they stopped talking and simply enjoyed their ride. Brenna closed her eyes and mulled over her enigmatic driver.

Once they arrived in Ellsworth, Jonathan didn't take the main street into the heart of town. At first she thought he was going to stop at the boarding house but he drove past that street too. She was just on the verge of asking where he was taking her when he stopped the car in front of a small two-story house with diamond-paned windows and swirling tendrils of clinging ivy.

"I'd like you to meet someone," he said as he leaped from the car and walked around to open her door.

"Oh . . . is this the business you had to attend to?" she asked, truly puzzled that he would want her to tag along.

Jonathan grabbed her arm and led her up the few stairs to the front door.

"I thought it was time you met Em. I told her all about you and you must be curious yourself."

Brenna was stunned. She couldn't believe he had the audacity to introduce her to his girl friend. She stood stiffly beside him as he opened the front door without knocking, nudging Brenna to enter ahead of him.

"Em . . . Em . . . it's me, Jonathan."

A large tabby cat pranced to the doorway and stood glaring up at them.

"She must be in the parlor," he said as he urged the reluctant woman along.

Brenna walked into the parlor and immediately felt like a fool. Seated in a love seat was a woman who had to be at least seventy years old.

"Em," he said softly, "I'd like you to meet Brenna Bryant, the apprentice I told you about. Brenna, this is my Great-Aunt Emmeline."

The old woman's crinkly frail brown skin glowed as she smiled at her great-nephew. "Oh, Jonny, you did make it after all. I'm so pleased. Come, sit down."

Brenna sat next to the old woman while Jonathan pulled up a chair. The pictures on the parlor walls were reminiscent of those in her room in Jonathan's house.

"Jonny's told me so much about you, Brenna," she said informally, "but he didn't tell me you were such a beauty."

The younger woman was too overwhelmed to speak. First she had learned Jonathan's "girl friend" was really his great-aunt and then she heard that he spoke of her even though, until today, he hadn't had anything to say to *her* at all.

Jonathan smiled, slightly embarrassed. "I must have forgotten, Em."

"Nonsense. One doesn't forget a pretty face. What's the matter? Your eyes going bad?" she said saucily. "Best you get your nose out of those blue-prints for a while and see the beauty around you."

It was so humorous to watch this frail woman cause her strapping great-nephew to squirm in his seat. Brenna couldn't contain her laughter.

"What's so funny?" he drawled.

She was beyond caring. "You!"

"Now don't give her your threatening tone," Em said firmly. She turned to the young girl beside her. "It's just an act anyway," she whispered loud enough for her great-nephew to hear.

"Really, Em!"

Em insisted on fixing a pot of tea and she brought out a plate of applesauce cookies too. They sat around and ate while Em told little anecdotes about her favorite great-nephew—much to his embarrassment.

"Yes, I can remember when my brother's son first brought his wife and family home to Maine for a visit," she said, misty-eyed. "Now the girls didn't take to the quiet too much but Jonny, he took to the countryside like a duck to water."

Brenna helped herself to another cookie, realizing how little she really knew about her employer.

"You look surprised, Brenna," the old woman said, as she rested her slightly gnarled hands in her lap.

"Oh . . . it isn't anything, Em. It's just that I didn't realize Jonathan had a family. I meant to say . . ."

Brenna cast a glance in his direction, amused to find a look of mock horror on his face.

"Did you think I was hatched from an egg?" he said, feigning indignation. "Or do you suppose I was left on someone's doorstep?"

Great-Aunt Emmeline cackled and patted Brenna's hand. "Don't let my great-nephew get you in a dither," she said. "I know exactly what you mean. You thought he was an only child, is that it? It's his arrogant ways, I'm afraid. Even when he was a scrawny child, he walked around as if he owned the roost. Although I know for certain his three older sisters used to beat him up to keep him in line."

Jonathan looked heavenward and shook his head. "I'm afraid it was the only means I could think of to keep those three wildcats off my back," he chuckled. "If I acted tough, they weren't certain that *I wouldn't* beat them up in return."

Jonathan a scrawny child? Brenna could not imagine that. His long muscular denim-clad legs stretched out before him, making the parlor seem smaller than it actually was. One large brown hand easily engulfed his teacup. No, it was difficult to imagine such a virile man as a weakling whom his sisters could beat up.

Jonathan casually glanced at his watch, then un-
wound his tall frame from his chair.

"I'm afraid we have to be going, Em," he said.
"Brenna has some shopping to do and I have to call
Nathan about the work on the house."

The old woman rose from the love seat and
grasped the younger woman's arm, escorting her to
the door.

"I'm very glad you came to visit, Jonny, and thank
you for bringing Brenna along, too." They stopped at
the front door and the old woman hurried off into the
kitchen, returning with a brown paper bag.

"Here's some applesauce cookies for later," she
said. "Now you bring this girl back again, you hear,
Jonny?"

Jonathan took the bag from his great-aunt and a
boyish smile crossed his lips. "Yes, Em, I'll bring her
back. I promise."

Em brushed Brenna's cheek with her lips, then
poked her great-nephew in his chest with one frail
finger.

"Behave yourself," she said firmly.

Like a little boy Jonathan nodded, casting Brenna a
furtive look to see her response to the scene between
his great-aunt and himself. The tall man stooped
quickly and planted a kiss on Em's cheek. She in turn
patted the side of his face lovingly, then shooed them
both out the door.

As they pulled away from the house, the old
woman stood in the doorway waving good-bye.
Brenna waved in return and Jonathan gave several
honks on the horn.

"She's fantastic," Brenna sighed, hating to leave
the old woman behind. Jonathan agreed.

"Em is a remarkable woman. You know she'll be eighty-five on her next birthday and she's still going strong."

"I can't believe she'll be eighty-five," Brenna said quickly to dispel the heavy mood that had overtaken him. "I thought she was, at the very most, seventy."

Jonathan smiled. "Em always said it was the clean Maine air that kept her young. Even though my father tried to get her to come to Philadelphia for a long visit, the most she would stay was two weeks. She doesn't like to be away from her home too long."

"Isn't it lonely for her in that house?" Brenna asked. "I assume that your great-uncle—her husband —is gone?"

A somber look fleetingly passed his face. "Yes, Uncle Edward died several winters ago. I tried to get Em to live with me in Bar Harbor but she doesn't like the tourist crowd that invades the area. She'd rather stay in the house she and Uncle Edward shared for nearly sixty years."

"So you try to see her as often as you can?"

Jonathan nodded. "Or at least try to talk her into spending some time with me in Bar Harbor. You're staying in the room I decorated for her." This news hadn't surprised Brenna. She had thought the photos were familiar. "By the way, I'm glad you and Em hit it off. For a moment I thought you wouldn't. You didn't seem thrilled about meeting her when you got out of the car."

Doesn't anything get by him, she wondered. "That was because I thought she was your . . . I mean I didn't realize I was going to meet anyone."

Jonathan parked the car and gave her a knowing look. "You thought Em was my girl friend?"

Brenna looked nervously out the window. Her silence was confirmation enough; Jonathan's laughter told her so.

"That explains why you screwed up your face every time I got a call from her," he teased.

"I did not screw up my face," she replied haughtily.

"Yes, you did . . . just like you're doing now."

Her hand flew to her face and they both laughed.

"Well, if I did screw up my face, I apologize," she said tentatively. "I'm not certain I know exactly what I thought," she lied, even though she knew the cat was out of the bag. "But your Em is a wonderful person and I'm glad I met her. I hope I didn't subconsciously misjudge you."

Jonathan turned in his seat and pushed her sunglasses atop her head. "Did I subconsciously misjudge you too?" He spoke solemnly and looked her directly in the eyes.

"I'm not engaged, if that's what you mean. It's been over . . ." He pressed his fingertips against her lips and halted her words. "You don't have to talk about it now. When you're ready."

Brenna studied him a moment, then put her sunglasses back in place.

"Do you want anything?" she asked, stepping from the car.

"No . . . but take your time."

She hurried into the store, feeling confused yet excited at the same time. She maneuvered up and down the aisles, her hand automatically reaching out for what she needed, for her eyes kept drifting to the front picture window where Jonathan could clearly be seen, leaning casually against the hood of her car, a cigarette in hand, a contemplative expression on his face.

The aroma of barbecue greeted Brenna and Jonathan upon their return to their Bar Harbor base and they followed the delicious scent to the patio where Michael presided over four thick steaks, corn, and baked potatoes.

"I hoped you two would be back in time to join Elaine and me for an early dinner," Michael said casually, making it sound as if the "two" of them went out often. Nevertheless, Brenna could not deny her pleasure that her time with this amicable Jonathan would last longer.

"There's a pitcher of strawberry daiquiris in the cooler." Michael gestured to a red and white box atop the patio table.

"Sounds good to me, Mike." Jonathan turned his ebullient gaze on Brenna. "How about you?"

A cool drink sounded good to Brenna and she subconsciously flicked her tongue across her lips in anticipation, a gesture that captured Jonathan's attention, causing the light in his eyes to darken and smoulder for an instant.

"Sounds wonderful to me, too. I am thirsty." Brenna took the seat Jonathan held out for her. His nearness sent a sudden tingling up the nape of her neck. "Where's Elaine?" she asked somewhat hoarsely to her own ears.

The sound of sliding glass doors caught everyone's attention and a petite honey blonde, carrying a bowl of salad, joined them.

"Jonathan . . . Brenna . . . I'd like you to meet

Elaine Edwards, my fiancée," Michael beamed taking the bowl from her.

"Why Michael . . ." Brenna stammered, a familiar feeling wrenching her heart, ". . . congratulations."

Jonathan poured daiquiris for everyone, aware of a certain sadness in Brenna's eyes.

"We've only been engaged for a few months," Elaine's rich laughter filled the air. "I think Michael and I are still getting used to our new status," she said. Her luminous eyes glowed with happiness, reminding Brenna how she once looked upon Clifton with similar happiness and joy in her own heart.

"Here's to many years of happiness." Jonathan's toast saved the moment. He was curious about Brenna's sudden sullenness.

"Have you set a date for the wedding yet?" Brenna asked, suddenly aware of Jonathan's scrutiny.

"No, not yet," Elaine replied taking a seat. "I'm a first-year law student in New York. Unfortunately we don't know where Michael will be working yet."

Michael squeezed his fiancée's shoulder. "Hopefully, not too far away."

Dinner was a huge success, with Michael agilely including Elaine in their conversation. It was clear she adored him and that the feeling was mutual. No matter how Brenna tried she couldn't squash the memory of her once-perfect love from her mind. She was jealous of what Michael and Elaine obviously shared and as soon as the opportunity presented itself she escaped to the kitchen for a respite from the happy couple.

"They make quite a pair, don't they?" Jonathan opened the sliding screen door and joined her. He stuffed the trash he was carrying into a plastic bag and tied the top closed.

"Yes, they make quite an attractive couple. I love her Boston accent." Brenna pulled out the silverware drawer.

"Do you have any plans for tomorrow?" Jonathan asked.

"No . . . no I don't." Brenna's breathing quickened.

"I plan to climb to the summit tomorrow. Would you care to join me?"

Brenna picked up four spoons for the dessert and closed the drawer.

"I'll take care of our lunch," Jonathan added quickly. "We can take our time in case you don't feel you're quite up to it."

"I'd love to go hiking with you, Jonathan," she replied, wondering if it were possible that he was unsure of himself as she.

"Good. Then it's settled." His beaming smile burned Brenna's earlier unhappiness from her thoughts.

After they ate Elaine's homemade strawberry ice cream, Michael took Elaine back to her hotel in Bar Harbor. "Don't wait up," he said cheerfully.

"We won't see him again until Elaine is on her way back to Boston," Jonathan whispered, his implication quite clear.

Brenna cleared the patio table, ignoring his comment, although she too had gotten the distinct feeling all evening that Michael couldn't wait to have the beautiful lawyer-to-be to himself.

The remainder of the evening was wonderful and totally unexpected. Brenna and Jonathan played several games of backgammon and then Jonathan attempted to teach her chess. Unfortunately, she was miserable at the latter and he had no problem beating her in six moves. Brenna felt like an imbecile and vowed to get herself a beginner's book on chess.

"Don't worry," he said, gently tugging a strand of her hair. "I've got until summer's end to whip your game into shape."

He pulled her to him gently and Brenna felt the pounding of her heart in her head. Jonathan's lips were soft and persuasive as he nibbled her lower lip, then slowly vanquished her mouth with his probing tongue. She held onto the front of his shirt while her thoughts raced madly through her head. It was as if he were picking up from where they left off four weeks ago and a niggling fear slowly crept through her veins. His earlier rejection of her had wounded more than Brenna wished to admit and she had only known him for a few days. If she permitted him to assume that all was forgiven, there was no telling how this night would end or what condition her heart and emotions would be in come morning. She couldn't take the chance. She *wouldn't* take the chance, for Brenna realized Jonathan had the power to devastate her as no other human being ever had.

Reluctantly, she pulled away, steeling herself for his response.

"Tired?"

He had thrown her a straw and she grabbed for it. "Yes, it's been a long day." Turning her back to him, she picked up their wine glasses and the cheese and cracker tray.

"Are you certain there isn't something else bothering you?"

She was glad her back was to him, hiding her face from his inquisitive eyes. Jonathan gently held her shoulders and nuzzled her neck. "Of course, Jonathan, I'm sure," she lied.

Without turning her around to face him, Jonathan took the tray and glasses from her with one hand and wrapped an arm beneath her breasts. "You'd better get some sleep then. We have a big day tomorrow." She was certain he could feel her speeding heart now, but he didn't mention it. Jonathan kissed a slow trail from the side of her neck, to her earlobe and cheek, compelling her to yield her mouth for one last questing kiss.

"Good night, Brenna."

"Night, Jonathan," she whispered, and she climbed the stairs to her room on trembling legs.

Nighttime had not quite slipped away when Brenna restlessly threw the covers aside, pulling on her short satin kimono-styled robe over the equally short nightdress. She had the urge for a hot cup of coffee and opened the hope chest at the foot of her bed where she placed her emergency travel bag. In it she kept a little of everything: mad money, needle and thread, Band-Aids, small vile of antiseptic, safety pins, and a hot coil with packets of instant coffee, creamer, and sugar. The water from the bathroom faucet was steaming so she took a cautious sip of her drink before stepping out onto the verandah. A pale gray light blanketed the skies but the night sounds were fading, replaced by one lone chirping bird, then another and another until Brenna had nearly finished her coffee as dawn's first light peaked over the summit.

Jonathan hadn't intended to walk around the

house via the verandah but he had felt restless all night which was unusual for him. He simply wanted to shake the feeling from his body. Maybe have a cigarette. He was completely taken aback then when he turned the corner and found Brenna staring in awe of the coming sun. A rising breeze blew her hair and opened her robe exposing her from her long slender neck to her lithe legs beneath her short nightgown. He remembered one of his sisters had gotten a similar outfit for Christmas a few years ago and had proudly modeled it for the other girls, much to his embarrassment. Now looking at Brenna in the same outfit he didn't feel embarrassed at all. No . . . not at all.

"Good morning," he said, walking toward her. "Sleep well?"

"Oh, Jonathan!" Brenna jumped, sloshing the coffee over her hand.

"Oh, Good Lord! I've done it again." He pulled a head bandanna from his back pocket. "I've got this knack for scaring you half to death." He took the cup from her hand and placed it on the railing, then dried her hand and wiped off the cuff of her sleeve.

He was already dressed in a sweatshirt, jeans, and hiking boots, making her aware of her state of undress.

"I hope I'm not holding things up this morning," she said, stuttering slightly. "I guess I was more tired than I thought."

He waved his hand and shrugged his shoulders. "No problem, we have the entire day. Are you hungry?"

She nodded yes.

"Good, I haven't eaten yet so I'll fix two of *my* famous bachelor omelets."

"Sounds good to me."

Jonathan looked down at the stream below.

"Do you have hiking boots?"

"No, but I do have a pair of sneakers," she said, hoping they would be sufficient.

"They'll have to do. And you better wear some long pants," he suggested turning to face her once more.

Brenna flushed at his open observation and pulled her robe tightly around her. Her breath caught in her throat and she watched him saunter toward her. He placed one hand behind her head, the other on her hip, then lazily pulled her to him, softly brushing her lips with his. Before she could decide what to do, whether to return his embrace or not, he let her go.

"I'd better start those omelets. See you downstairs."

Her legs shook slightly as she watched him amble away. The aching need her restless sleep hadn't subdued burned anew.

Jonathan's "bachelor omelet" turned out to be a monstrous though tasty concoction of eggs, onion, bacon, mushrooms, green peppers, and a couple of slices of tomato on the side. After they had eaten, Brenna cleared away the dishes while Jonathan prepared a knapsack. Before the sun was at its zenith they were on their way, falling into an easy pace as Jonathan led the way upstream. She had walked the path many times before but unexpectedly Jonathan veered off the path and started up a gradual incline through a cluster of red pine and pungent balsam fir trees.

Occasionally he turned around to see how she was faring, offering a smile of encouragement or a helping hand when necessary. He pointed out a "hobbit" world of tiny growing things; mushrooms of every shape and possible color peppered the forest floor as well as tiny seedlings of spruce, wild lily of the valley, and mountain cranberry.

"Do you want to stop for a breather?"

They had walked for nearly forty minutes. Brenna wasn't particularly tired since their pace was slow but, although she enjoyed the hike, there was something eerie about the shadowed world about them. The trees were so thick in areas that their branches blocked most of the sun.

"No, Jonathan, I'm fine."

He nodded and continued his upward progress. Brenna couldn't help but be aware of his taut thighs against his jeans as he stalked ahead of her and the sureness of his step. He had traveled this way many times before, she was certain. The chatter of birds and the rustlings of chipmunks were peaceful company; then a crashing in the trees overhead startled Brenna, who looked skyward and promptly lost her footing, plummeting down the embankment.

She lay still while she tried to get her bearings. Then a faint sound of splitting twigs pierced her consciousness. Two strong arms rolled her over onto her back and a pair of dark concerned eyes swept over her.

"Brenna, are you all right?" Jonathan's breathing was labored from chasing her rolling body down the hill.

She gazed, bewildered, into his eyes while he brushed her hair out of her face. "I'm fine, Jonathan . . . really," she stammered but when she tried to sit up he pushed her back down into the bed of moss and grass.

"Stay still."

"But I'm fine . . ."

"Be quiet and do what I say," he reprimanded.

Carefully he checked both her arms and legs for broken bones. Brenna was touched by his concern but felt embarrassed by her klutziness. For the first time she noticed a trace of perspiration on his brow. Satisfied that she had not broken anything, he sat down beside her and scooped her up in his arms, gently plucking the twigs from her hair.

"It was only a pair of flying squirrels," Jonathan sighed heavily.

"What?"

"Flying squirrels . . . in the trees." He cocked his head and motioned to the trees above them. She could barely identify two creatures soaring from branch to branch, but she could feel the slowing beat of his heart beneath the palm of her hand as she rested against him.

"I just looked up for a second . . . next thing I knew I was falling."

He took a handkerchief from his back pocket and brushed the dirt off her face.

"Well, the next time you decide to look up," he said, "stop walking first." Jonathan's eyes sparkled at his jest. Brenna laughed, then took the handkerchief from him and dried his moist brow.

"Are you trying to tell me I can't chew gum and walk at the same time?" she said impishly.

"Something like that." He smiled openly, showing even white teeth.

She closed her eyes, basking in the warmth from the semi-dark glade, secure in the circle of Jonathan's arms. For a time they sat quietly; then she felt feathery light kisses on her eyelids. His arms loosened their hold and Jonathan gently caressed the sides of her arms and her back. Hesitantly she opened her eyes in time to see his head lower. He slowly drank from her lips, covering her mouth with his own. Brenna reveled in his caress and her hands, once splayed against his chest, circled his waist. She massaged her fingertips into his lower back. Jonathan moaned. Emboldened by his response, she continued her exploration; spurred on by her actions, his gentle kisses turned voracious. Deftly he opened her mouth with his tongue and ravaged the sweetness within.

Her mind whirled as she remembered that first night in Bar Harbor so long ago. She had forgotten how good Jonathan felt, how his hands could wreak havoc with her body. Easing her back on the ground, Jonathan cushioned her head with his arm and stretched out beside her, covering half her body with his own. He kissed her mouth hungrily and Brenna was lost. Her hands rose up underneath his sweatshirt and she tickled his sides and back with her fingertips. It wasn't until she felt his hand tenderly cupping her breast that she realized that Jonathan had pushed up her shirt and unfastened her bra. His breath came in ragged gasps and Brenna was well aware of his own state of arousal. When his tongue flicked across one nipple, Brenna knew she had to stop him or be lost forever.

"Jonathan . . . no," she whispered huskily. He

continued his touches for a moment, then grasped her hips tightly and froze in position. The tranquility of the glade seemed filled with their labored breathing. Jonathan pulled her top down and buried his head in the hollow of her covered breasts. Regaining his control, he raised himself on one elbow and looked at the woman beneath him.

"Remember when I asked you never to be afraid of me?" he said evenly.

She looked pleadingly into his eyes. "Yes . . . yes I do but . . ."

"I want you, Brenna, and I think you want me too."

Jonathan looked at her questioningly, "You do trust me?"

"Perhaps it isn't you I don't trust," she offered, knowing how true that statement was.

Releasing a quaking sigh, he held her tightly for a moment, then kissed her forehead. "I think you need some time," he said abruptly, as he raised himself to a sitting position and helped her up too.

"Yes . . . some time."

He smiled at her reassuringly, then reached behind her and refastened her bra. The intimacy of the act excited her more.

"Do you want to continue the hike?" he asked as he buttoned her blouse and helped her to her feet.

"Yes . . . if you're still up to it."

"Oh, I'm more than up to it." He placed his knapsack on his back. "I have to do something to work off this energy I've suddenly developed."

Before she could die of embarrassment, Jonathan planted a sound kiss on her lips, grabbed her hand, and proceeded up the embankment with a light-headed Brenna in tow.

The two walked in companionable silence as Jonathan showed her the world he dearly loved. The trail dipped in and out among the trees until they came across a pond with a very active beaver community. They watched quietly until they were spotted. The loud thump of a beaver's tail warned the others of intruders and sent them all scurrying from sight.

"I wish I'd brought my camera," she said.

"We'll come back again," he promised and squeezed her hand as they continued their journey, until the trees thinned and Brenna found herself atop a summit.

"Here we are."

Jonathan removed his knapsack and sat down, his back against a rock formation. Brenna sat down beside him.

"It's beautiful, Jonathan," she said.

Before them was a breathtaking view of Mount Desert Island. In the distance was the town of Bar Harbor. Below them was the woodland they had just trekked through and beyond that the Atlantic Ocean, dotted with sailing craft.

"Do you come here often?" she asked as he offered her a sandwich.

"As often as I can. It's a good place to think." He peeked in his knapsack and pulled out a beer for himself and a soft drink for her.

"It might still be a little frozen. I put it in the freezer last night."

She smiled. "You thought of everything, I see."

He put an arm about her shoulders. "I admit I was a Boy Scout and I *do* believe in being prepared."

"Everything looks so right, Jonathan." She liked the feel of him and the smell of his cologne.

"Hmmmm . . . the birds and animals have the forests and ponds and we get to share a little of the beauty with them. Everything has its place."

Brenna whispered, "I wish I could find my place."

She wasn't certain this was the time to tell him about Clifton but she supposed there would never be a perfect time. Jonathan thirstily downed his beer and lit a cigarette.

"Don't stop now. Talk to me," he encouraged.

Brenna wet her dry lips. "A year ago I thought my place was with Clifton Richards."

"The guy who gave you the ring?"

She told Jonathan of Clifton and their early courtship. And about how long it had taken her to realize Clifton was trying to run her life for her regardless of what she wanted to do. Jonathan remained silent as she spoke of her year abroad, the letters—or lack of them—and the emotionless ending of their engagement. He listened to every word, then turned in her direction.

"Do you still love him?"

I don't love him. But I could easily fall in love with you.

She grasped her can of soda tightly and looked away from his piercing stare. It took a second for her to accept what her subconsciousness had already known and obviously accepted.

"No . . . that's behind me now."

Jonathan collected their garbage and stowed it away in his knapsack. He helped her to her feet, stopping to caress her cheek.

"Perhaps this summer will help you find your place," he said cryptically and he took her hand and led the way from the summit.

CHAPTER SIX

Jonathan took his apprentices lobstering earlier in the day. But after a few hours on the cold waters throwing out traps and then harvesting three lobsters for their dinner, they had all looked forward to returning to the comfort of their summer home. A bright, crackling fire warmed the living room and Brenna contentedly curled up on the sofa after their succulent dinner, closed the novel she had been reading to watch the two men lost in their silent battle of chess. Since Jonathan had first attempted to teach her the game a month ago, Brenna had gone into Bar Harbor and bought a book on the subject which she read from cover to cover. Although she still wasn't a fantastic player, it now took Jonathan more than six moves to beat her, so she felt she had made some improvement.

Brenna observed Michael's move with a beginner's eye. His queen was positioned shrewdly for a possible check. But she was certain Jonathan's king had an evasive option to avoid mate. Nevertheless, it was obvious Michael was pleased and, glancing in her direction, he gave Brenna a conspiratory wink.

In the past few weeks Brenna, Michael, and Jonathan had gotten along better than she could have wished. Their working hours were far more flexible because they were ahead of schedule on the project.

Their camaraderie soon developed into a natural friendship and the next time Elaine had come to visit, Jonathan insisted she use the extra bedroom—to Michael's obvious delight. The foursome consequently spent that entire weekend together barbecuing, sailing, or just lazing about with an occasional game of team Trivial Pursuit in the evening. Brenna sighed. She knew she was accumulating pleasant memories of her stay in Maine. She also knew that most of the memories were centered around her host.

Ever since she met Jonathan's Great-Aunt Emmeline and the first hike together, Jonathan had changed toward her. He was more attentive and infinitely patient. And, although they had shared several embraces since their encounter in the glade, he had been careful not to rush and overwhelm her.

Unfortunately, ever since Brenna had admitted to herself that her feelings for him were not strictly professional, she found herself not wanting to keep him at bay. Sometimes a single fleeting glance in her direction or a casual caress would send her body trembling. But her common sense prevailed. She had no clear idea how he perceived her or what, if anything, he truly felt for her outside of a physical attraction. She kept reminding herself of her recent broken engagement. Had she recovered enough from that disappointment and disillusionment to trust her perspective of this situation? Yet, when she reconsidered, she told herself they had more in common than mere—for lack of a better word—lust. She truly believed he enjoyed her company as much as she enjoyed his. And, of course, they had the same love of architecture as well. But what if she were wrong about him? What if she had imagined everything? So, undecided, she was determined to hold her emotions in check.

Glancing at the clock on the mantle, Brenna stifled a yawn. Nathan Hammond had invited them to take a weekend holiday and spend the next four days enjoying the Rockland, Maine, Seafood Festival. He was providing his sloop for transportation and, if she hoped to get up early the next morning, she knew she'd better get some sleep.

Michael rose from his seat and changed the selection of albums on the stereo. A trumpet's melodious wail filtered through Brenna's consciousness and each lyrical refrain of Wynton Marsalis's music brought back the memory of the fevered caresses she and Jonathan had shared on the plush shag at her feet on the very first night she had spent in his home. She shivered slightly, recalling too the angry accusations he had leveled at her when he assumed she had been hiding her engagement from him. But that misunderstanding was behind them. They had become so companionable that she couldn't believe they had ever *not* spoken to one another. Not shared confidences as they did now.

A growing warmth spread over her and Brenna vividly recalled once more that long ago June evening. Finally rousing herself from her reveries, she glanced toward the men and found Michael contemplating his next move while Jonathan, his expression sensuously smoldering, was directed at her. She knew he must be remembering, too.

"I think I'll turn in," she said hastily, feeling flushed from head to toe. "We've a big day tomorrow."

Rising from the sofa, she picked up empty glasses and snack trays and exited to the kitchen. She took her time cleaning up, giving her racing heart the opportunity to slow to a normal pace. She admonished herself for her hasty departure. How could one look affect her so? And, determined to redeem herself by offering a final—controlled—good night, she returned to the living room. Jonathan, however, was nowhere to be seen.

"Good night, Michael."

"G'night, Brenna." Michael put the last of the chessmen into the velour-cushioned box. "Tonight Jonathan made the fatal move," he informed her triumphantly, "and it's about time, too. This is the first time I've beaten him in seven games. I was beginning to think I'd lost my touch."

Brenna wondered where Jonathan had disappeared to. Perhaps he had gone for a walk. If he had, he obviously wanted to be alone and, reluctant to seek him out, she trudged up the spiral staircase. She had just reached the landing and turned to her room when she bumped into the subject of her thoughts.

"Jonathan," she gasped, "I thought you went for a walk."

"Not until I say good night to you properly." His eyes were seductively slumberous, *"then* I'll go for a walk," he chuckled, "a very brisk one."

She glided effortlessly into his outstretched arms, moved that the music had obviously affected him as much as it had her. He held her gently, at first, then backed Brenna away from the stairs into the shadows. She responded eagerly to his kisses, even as he pressed her against the wall, his arms stretched out above her head, his lean body firmly entrenched against her warm supple curves. Brenna wound her arms about his neck, pressing herself ever closer as the familiar longing grew within her. Finally, he pulled his lips from hers and rested his forehead in the hollow of her neck.

"Tell me you don't want me," he whispered.

Brenna wasn't ready to reveal her feelings on that subject. Instead she tickled his sides, forcing him to muffle his laughter and quipped, "I don't want you."

Jonathan bit her earlobe in retaliation. "Liar." She heard the quiver in his voice, revealing his emotional state. How long could she put him off? Jonathan worked hard and played just as hard. He simply wasn't the type of man to relinquish his pleasures for too long.

"I think you'd better go to bed, lady." He kissed her on the forehead and turned her in the direction of her room. "While I'm still able to let you go— alone." Jonathan playfully swatted her backside before melting into the darkness. Brenna closed her bedroom door, still unable to believe the effect he had on her and the fact that she was able to arouse him so. And still undecided what she was going to do about it.

"Brenna. Brenna. Let's get moving!" Michael pounded on her door. "Elaine's meeting us in Rockland and you *know* I don't want to keep her waiting."

Brenna chuckled at Michael's impatience but it was contagious. She pulled a peach-colored sundress quickly over her head and checked the shoulder ties for length. Giving her hair a few brisk strokes, she tossed her brush on the vanity and fitted a pair of gold saucer earrings in her lobes and a choker about her throat. They had all agreed to forgo breakfast this morning in order to get an early start. Brenna had volunteered to fix a large thermos of hot coffee and pack pastry for the 154-mile trip to Rockland.

Satisfied that she looked presentable, Brenna grabbed her shawl and bag and hurried down the stairs. She heard Michael's and Jonathan's voices outside the house and, leaving her bag in the foyer, she headed for the kitchen. Brenna was oblivious to everything but her task. The coffee was percolating and would be ready in minutes. Reaching into the overhead cabinets she located the large thermos. She had just finished pouring the hot liquid into the container when she felt warm kisses along her shoulder blades and two strong arms about her waist.

"Is that you, Jonathan?" she said drolly.

Jonathan chuckled, then pulled her back against him. "And who else would it be?" he challenged, lifting her hair to nibble the back of her neck.

"Oh, a friendly bear . . . lost stranger . . . Michael. You know."

Jonathan gave her his own definition of a bear hug, then released her. Leaning against the counter, he eyed her wickedly.

"You know that you're playing with fire, don't you?"

Ignoring his remark, she capped the thermos, carefully placing it in the picnic hamper next to a carton of orange juice, pastry, and cups.

"Has the sloop arrived yet?"

"It should be here any moment. Are you ready?"

"Almost. I just need to retrieve my suitcase in the foyer." She turned to look at him finally and her breath caught in her throat. For the past two months, she had seen him in his usual uniform of tight jeans and shirt. Even when Elaine had visited, his attire hadn't changed. Now, however, he stood before her in a navy blue short-sleeved safari shirt and matching slacks.

"You look lovely," he said, his eyes intent on her hidden form.

"So do you," she said inanely. Jonathan laughed.

"The sloop is here!" Michael shouted through the kitchen window.

"You bring the food and I'll get your bag," Jonathan instructed.

Grasping the hamper and purse, Brenna opened the back door, trying to contain her exhilaration when the telephone shrilled. Placing the hamper on the counter, she picked up the wall phone. "Hello, Maxwell residence," she said gaily.

"Hello . . . hello, Brenna? Is that you?"

She recognized a familiarity in the voice. "Why, yes . . . this is Brenna Bryant." Suddenly it dawned on her who was on the other end of the call.

"Hi, honey. It's me, Clifton."

Her knees nearly buckled beneath her and she reached for the counter for support. "Clifton! How did you know where to reach me?" *Why are you calling me now,* she wanted to shout.

"I ran into your old roomy, Catharine. She told me where I could reach you," he explained. "I have to talk to you, Brenna," he added quietly.

Brenna's mind raced furiously. What *did* he want from her? Why did her ex-roommate tell Clifton where he could find her?

"Brenna? Hurry up." The voice came from outside

the house. But was it Michael's voice or Jonathan who called.

"I have to go, Clifton," she said bluntly.

"But I need to speak with you," he pleaded.

"I'm on my way out . . . I can't talk now."

"You could, if you wanted to," he said petulantly. "I love you. We need to talk."

Brenna winced. How could he say he loved her after all that had passed between them? After all this time? Yes, they had to talk but Brenna was certain he wouldn't like what she had to say. "All right, Clifton, we'll talk but I must go now."

"Promise me you'll call," he pressed.

"Yes, Clifton, I'll call you as soon as I can," she promised. Anything to get off the phone! She hung up without saying good-bye. Brenna sighed with relief and retrieved her bag and hamper just in time to see Jonathan's retreating form through the kitchen window.

Usually when the threesome traveled together, they didn't have any difficulty making conversation. But the leisure trip to Rockland was made in unusual silence. And, after a few abortive attempts to elicit more than a monosyllabic response from his companions, Michael retreated to the bow to sit by the captain who kept him entertained with a running commentary of their surroundings. The sloop passed through the Cranberry Isles, then headed southwest, swinging north of Swans Island through Jericho Bay. Since Nathan wasn't expecting them until late afternoon, Billy, their skipper, who was working for Hammond for the summer months, navigated toward Isle au Haut, a beautiful island only six miles long and three miles wide, but renowned in the area for its magnificent cliffs that towered five hundred feet or more, rising like sentinels from the deep turbulent waters below.

The sheer beauty of the ageless cliffs finally seized Brenna's attention from her ex-fiancé. A sudden surge of anger gripped her for a split second. Here she was, on a sleek forty-foot sloop, skimming through the water, surrounded by breathtaking scenery and she wasn't enjoying it. Brenna determined then and there that, although she didn't know why Clifton was trying to get back into her life, she was certain of one fact: *she* didn't love *him.* Perhaps she never really had. A disturbing and sobering thought for she had known Clifton far longer than she had known Jonathan and what she felt for Jonathan was deeper than anything she experienced with Clifton, she was certain. Nevertheless, she would not permit the morning's telephone call to intrude and ruin the four-day holiday that lay ahead of her.

Her mind made up she turned to Jonathan. "They're pretty fantastic," she said, indicating the cliffs they were now leaving behind.

"So. You finally noticed." Jonathan's eyes were hidden behind his dark sunglasses but his tone of voice barely concealed his displeasure. For the first time that day, she realized she hadn't said more than a few words to him since they departed that morning.

"I'm sorry, Jonathan. My mind was elsewhere." She gave him her best smile. "I guess I haven't been much company."

He gave no answering smile, no hint of understanding. His lips were a taut thin line of accusation.

"You probably had something more important on your mind . . . or someone."

She was about to ask him to explain his cryptic response when Michael rejoined them, his enthusiasm for the trip and his offer to refill everyone's coffee cups taking over the moment.

You probably had something more important on your mind, he had said. *Or someone.* She repeated over to herself. *Someone? Someone!* Brenna nearly spilled her coffee. It was glaringly obvious. The distant voice outside the kitchen window while she dealt with Clifton's phone call. The sight of Jonathan's retreating form after she hung up the phone. Jonathan had heard her on the phone. But what exactly did he hear? Obviously not the entire conversation, otherwise he would know she had been less than delighted to hear from her ex-fiancé.

The trepidation she felt seeing Jonathan's displeasure quickly evaporated when Brenna realized he was jealous. Jonathan was jealous! Seeing him in this new light, her skin prickled with growing excitement. He was angry now but once she explained everything to him he would be her Jonathan once more. Perhaps the phone call had been a blessing in disguise. Brenna smiled but Jonathan, seeing the smile, scowled even more. Her heart lurched at the unhappiness in his eyes. The pain. The anger. But she couldn't explain now. Not with Michael so near. She'd have an opportunity to set things right, she told herself, just as soon as they reach Rockland and the house Nathan had rented for the weekend festivities.

By the time they reached Rockland, Jonathan's sullenness had not lifted and Brenna could barely wait to alight from the boat. The sloop was expertly navigated against the pier and Michael assisted her onto the dock while Jonathan had a few last words with the skipper. Walking across the platform to the stairs that hugged the side of the small cliff, Brenna spied Nathan trotting down to greet them.

"Brenna, good to see you," he said cheerfully, kissing her on the cheek. "And Michael." He grasped the younger man's hand. "How was the trip?"

"The best!" Michael replied.

"Jonathan, my boy, how are you?"

The presence of his old friend seemed to work wonders. Jonathan broke into a wide grin and commended Nathan for suggesting they travel by boat instead of driving. How could he be so enthusiastic about the boat ride when he hadn't said more than a few sentences to anyone the entire trip, Brenna thought, then shrugged, thankful that his moodiness had finally lifted.

"I hope you are all hungry," Nathan announced. "The cook has prepared lobster bisque and stuffed baked rainbow trout for lunch."

The four climbed the staircase, which brought them to the terrace that overlooked the ocean. A table had been set up for lunch and Godwin gestured that they all be seated.

"Have you heard from Elaine?" Michael asked anxiously.

"Oh, yes, please forgive me. She's inside freshening up," Nathan told him. "She's a lovely girl, Michael. Lovely."

"Uncle's right. She is lovely. We were just getting to know one another better," chimed a husky but definitely feminine voice.

Michael jumped up and quickly embraced his girl

friend, temporarily hiding the husky-voiced woman from view.

"Brenna. Michael. I'd like you to meet my niece, Monica Weathers."

Monica's greeting was cordial but brief. "Jonathan, you look marvelous," she said, turning all her attention to him.

Brenna watched the petite woman glide across the patio. Jonathan rose from his chair, accepting Monica's hands on his shoulders as she stood on tiptoe to plant a kiss on his lips.

"You look marvelous yourself, Monica," he replied gallantly.

While Monica and Jonathan bantered compliments about, Brenna assessed the woman in the diaphanous green floor-length robe that swirled about her, revealing a scandalous aqua maillot that was cut high, high up her hips and low everyplace else, leaving little to the imagination. Short curly hair framed her face, tapering down her neck and her eyes lit brightly as she openly flirted with Jonathan. Brenna's heart lodged in her throat as she took in Jonathan's answering smile. He seemed to be enjoying the woman's attention.

Michael glanced at Brenna briefly as he seated Elaine but she chose to ignore his questioning glance. Looking at Monica, Brenna couldn't help but feel that she'd seen the woman before. But where?

As if reading Brenna's thoughts, Michael said, "Excuse me Ms. Weathers . . ."

"Oh, call me Monica, please," she said airily, giving his arm a brotherly pat.

"All right, Monica. I know this is a cliché. But

haven't I seen you somewhere before?" he asked hesitantly.

Monica's laughter filtered through the air. She looked like the cat who swallowed the canary and, singing a cappella, repeated a well-known refrain from the Number-One song in the country prior to Brenna's departure for her year's study abroad. Nathan Hammond's niece was one-third of "Champagne" a bouncy, vivacious trio that was well-known for its suggestive lyrics and daring, scanty stage attire.

Michael beamed and Brenna could have cheerfully strangled him and Elaine for singing along with her. Everyone was laughing and having a wonderful time. Everyone but Brenna who had a premonition that this glorious holiday weekend wasn't going to live up to her expectations.

"Looks like the weekend is off to a wonderful start," Nathan applauded. "Now, anyone for a cocktail?"

"Uncle, this is a special occasion so I insist we all have champagne," Monica enthused.

"Sounds good to me," Jonathan said giving his stamp of approval which everyone else followed.

Godwin hurried off to fetch the champagne and Brenna tried to hide her confusion. Jonathan was so attentive to Nathan's niece that Brenna felt she might as well not exist. But she was determined not to put a damper on the festivities. She would just have to make the best of the situation despite the hurt and embarrassment that stabbed her relentlessly.

Glasses of champagne were quickly passed around.

"A toast," Nathan said. "To a marvelous four-day weekend . . . to us."

"Yes, to us," Monica echoed, her eyes riveted on Jonathan.

For the next thirty minutes Monica's laughter was the only sound Brenna heard. She tried to block it out, to concentrate and join in on the conversations that hovered about her but Brenna was too distraught to maintain her calm veneer much longer. She declined the offer of a second glass of champagne, pleading a headache.

"I'm sorry you're not feeling well, Brenna. I should have insisted you all rest after your journey." Nathan's concern made Brenna regret her little lie. But she had to get by herself for a while.

"I'll take a few aspirin," she reassured him. "I'm certain I'll feel better in no time."

In the safety of her room, Brenna flung herself on the bed, struggling to hold back the tears. The past four weeks had been so perfect between Jonathan and herself. They had seemed so attuned to one another. They loved their careers. They shared intimate moments, and, she admitted, she had secretly hoped he would fall in love with her as she had with him. Finally. It was out in the open. She had fallen in love with him and now the thought that her love would never be returned needled her heart. She had looked forward to this trip to Rockland and no doubt subconsciously hoped she and Jonathan would grow closer. But now those aspirations were dashed like the waves crashing against the rocky coastline.

How could Jonathan do this to her! How could he humiliate her in front of Nathan, not to mention Michael and Elaine. At that very moment Brenna

wished she had never heard of any contest *or* Rockland. She wished she had never come to Maine!

A knock on her bedroom door brought Brenna
quickly to a sitting position, drying her eyes on the
back of her hands.

"Uncle suggested I bring you these." Monica swept
into the room and, tossing Brenna a bottle of aspirin,
stretched out on the floral printed divan. "So you're
an architect, also?" she said, scrutinizing Brenna beneath her long-mascaraed lashes.

"I'm not a licensed architect yet," Brenna replied.
She leaned against the bedpost and returned the
woman's stare. "I still have to complete a three-year
apprenticeship."

Up close, Monica wasn't the effervescent nymph
she first appeared to be. Well-applied makeup hid
tiny lines at the corner of her eyes, concealed the
tightness about her mouth. She was definitely closer
to Jonathan's age than her own. Nevertheless,
Brenna had to admit the woman was attractive.

"And how does an apprenticeship work?"

"Usually one has to join an architectural firm to get
the necessary experience."

"Or work with a well-known architect on a one-on-
one basis?" Monica questioned, her almond-shaped
eyes narrowing into slits.

Brenna shrugged. "Whatever."

"I suppose you love working in Maine," the singer
probed.

Brenna wanted to say that she had enjoyed Maine
until she showed up but reconsidered. Too much
honesty could be disastrous.

"I think the countryside is beautiful and it certainly is peaceful here . . ."

Monica waved her hand limply. "Please spare me the travelogue. You're young . . . hmmmm . . . attractive, in your own way. Why would you want to bury yourself in Bar Harbor for an entire summer?"

Brenna seethed. Attractive in your own way indeed! "Architecture is my career. I was very fortunate to be offered this summer position. For your information, *Miss* Weathers, I . . ."

"Is everything all right, girls?" Nathan peeked his head around the door that Monica hadn't bothered to close completely.

"Oh, everything is fine, Uncle. Just a little girl-talk." Monica rose gracefully off the divan, slipping her arm through Hammond's.

"Do you feel any better, Brenna?"

"Oh I'm sure I will, Nathan, just as soon as I take two of these." Brenna stood and turned for the bathroom to get herself a glass of water. She really did have a headache now.

Brenna slept for over an hour before Godwin's knock on her door announced dinner. Feeling drained from her exhaustive nap instead of refreshed, Brenna tossed her baggage onto the bed, intent on finding the red off-the-shoulder floor-length sheath she had packed but never thought she'd have the occasion to wear. But she would wear the dress with the knee-high slash on the left side tonight. She needed all the confidence she could muster.

Dinner was a seafood-lover's delight. Mussels steeped in a tangy lemon sauce, lobster bisque, and stuffed trout graced the table and buffet. The food was exquisite and the conversation pleasant though strained. Whenever Brenna's eyes strayed to the blending heads of Jonathan and Monica, lost in quiet conversation, her speech faltered slightly. Whatever tasty morsel she was eating tasted like sand. Monica looked elegant in her simple but tasteful lavender silk caftan with the plunging neckline. And Jonathan was the perfect foil. His gray linen double-breasted blazer molded his shoulders, tapering gradually to his trim waist. The pearl-white silk shirt was a vivid contrast to his skin and jacket. And black linen trousers completed the picture of arresting, subtle masculinity.

They talked about the music industry for most of the meal, thanks to Monica who subtly manipulated the conversation. Brenna thought unkindly that the woman knew just what to say and just when to say it. Jonathan appeared contentedly titillated by her witty conversation and Elaine asked question after question about the record business. Still, though, she hated the sound of Monica's voice. She loathed a lull in conversation more. Those moments which Michael and Elaine used to steal a few quiet words. Those moments when Jonathan's head was bent close to Monica's, close enough that the singer took liberties, playfully straightening out the collar of his shirt. Or picking imaginary lint from his blazer. That left Nathan to entertain Brenna.

"I'm glad your headache hasn't ruined the evening for you," Nathan said.

"Yes, it's gone now. But I think I'll turn in early tonight just the same." *I think I've dealt with enough for one day.*

"That's probably the wisest thing to do," Monica concurred. The first direct words she had spoken to Brenna all evening. "All that wind, sun, and sea. I'm exhausted after an hour," she babbled. But no one seemed to care if she babbled or not—especially Jonathan.

Brenna poured herself another cup of coffee. "Actually, Monica, the trip was very pleasant. The nearby islands are beautifully remote . . . and the cliffs of Isle Au Haut . . ." The next twenty minutes were devoted to a spirited discussion about the area. Even Jonathan took his attention from his dinner partner to join in singing Maine's attributes. Monica was the only person seated at the table who didn't appreciate Brenna's asking question after question about this particular part of Maine. Her almond eyes were now narrow slits. Brenna didn't know what prompted her to alter the conversation, to wrest Monica from center stage. But the murderous look in the singer's eyes had been worth it.

Nathan eased away from the table. "Brandy, everyone?"

They adjourned to the richly paneled, book-lined den. Everyone had a brandy but Brenna. Too much had already happened to her today. She wasn't going to risk topping it off by mixing drinks and being ill. She had another cup of coffee.

"This house is lovely, Nathan," she said. "How did you ever manage to find this place for the holiday?" Nathan beamed. His eyes followed hers, seeing the study with its off-white walls and tan leather sofas through her appreciative eyes. Her eyes rested on a penciled portrait that had been propped on one shelf of the wall-to-wall entertainment center and bookcase. Brenna walked across the study to get a better look.

"A fair likeness of me, don't you think?" Nathan

joined her in front of the portrait. The character in Nathan's face was noticeably absent in the drawing. Still, it was obviously Nathan.

"It does look like you, Nathan," Brenna said honestly. "Who was the artist?"

"That's Monica's work." Brenna nearly gagged on her coffee. In the right-hand corner of the painting were the initials MW and the date. The drawing had been done two years ago.

"I did that drawing on Nathan's sloop," Monica said gaily. "But I think the one I did of Jonathan that day was my best. If it hadn't been for Mrs. Winslow, I would have completely forgotten about Uncle's drawing, which I'd left with some other things at the boarding house. Lucky for me that she found it and forwarded it along."

"Yes . . . that was lucky," Brenna said flatly.

"Monica was a fine-arts student at college," Jonathan revealed. "At least she was when we first met."

"But Monica was such a musical child," Nathan added, giving his niece an affectionate hug. "I wasn't really surprised when she turned to music."

"But I still like to keep my hand on my art." But, although Monica said art, Brenna felt keeping her hand on a certain architect was what the singer really had on her mind. It was clear that her relationship with Jonathan went back to their college days and only two years ago Monica and Jonathan vacationed together, she surmised. She might have mistaken Em for Jonathan's girl friend but if Monica wasn't currently filling that position, she was certainly staking a serious bid for it now. Well, she could have him, Brenna concluded.

"If you'll all excuse me," Brenna said, "I think I'll call it an evening."

Sleep had always held recuperative powers for Brenna. As a youngster, she would bury herself under the covers whenever she was upset or had a problem. Usually by morning she felt better, or at least had a more positive outlook on the source of her difficulties. This time was no exception. After bidding everyone good night, she fell into a deep restful sleep. So deep in fact that she didn't awaken until late the following morning, when bright sunlight streamed into her room.

The previous day's events flashed in Brenna's mind like a slide show and she stared at the ceiling. Finally, she rose from the bed and took a seat in front of the vanity mirror. She looked awful. Her eyes were puffy from too much sleep and her hair was a tangled mess. She tried not to think about Jonathan and the distance he had placed between them. She definitely didn't want to think about Monica who had known Jonathan far longer than she. The singer probably had many fond memories of him as well.

The possibility that she had been a diversion for the architect because she was living in his house and therefore was available all summer was too painful for Brenna to consider. She simply would not dwell on it. She *couldn't* dwell on it. She would enjoy this four-day weekend or at least pretend to even if it killed her, Brenna determined.

CHAPTER SEVEN

Saturday and Sunday passed in a haze of bewilderment and pain. Every place they went, Monica clung proprietarily to Jonathan's arm, leaving Nathan to be Brenna's escort. The elder man offered his assistance, just in case she needed to talk. But although Brenna was fond of Nathan—they had become close in the past few months—she had to keep in mind that Monica *was* his niece and Jonathan the son the childless widower always wished he had.

Despite her own unhappiness, however, Brenna's main concern was Nathan. She was certain the late nights and frenzied pace Monica was setting was tasking the elder man's health. Still, out of deference to her—so Brenna would not feel like a fifth wheel—he accompanied the younger people everywhere. After their third straight late night, however, Brenna decided to go off on her own and give Nathan at least one day's rest.

The next day, Brenna left a note for Nathan by his breakfast setting. She was taking him up on his generous offer, she had written, the use of his launch. Billy would take her to Matinicus Island and pick her up later. Stealing into the kitchen, Brenna packed herself a lunch, then hurried down to the pier where Billy waited. The trip to Matinicus, barely twenty miles away, was completed in no time at all. Billy dropped her off somewhere between the island's rugged eastern side and the long fields that sloped gently to the sea on the west. Brenna strolled about, soothed by the solitude. Matinicus was a lovely island that somehow managed to maintain its remoteness. At least here, she would find total peace—if only for a few hours.

Brenna trooped about the island exploring and taking pictures for several hours. When she tired of that, she found a spot and ate her lunch, then pulled out a paperback novel. Perhaps it was lack of sleep due to the late nights she'd been keeping lately or perhaps it was the strain she'd been under since her arrival in Rockland, for before she read one chapter Brenna fell into a sound sleep only to awaken several hours later to a cold, ominously dark sky and angry ocean. Disoriented at first, Brenna got her bearings and glanced at her wristwatch. It was passed the allotted time to meet Billy. She retraced her movements, hoping that he was still waiting for her at their designated rendezvous. A brief flash of lightning followed by rolling thunder startled her and she walked faster. When the sky displayed its rising anger once more and gusts of wind threw her off balance, she began to panic—was she going in the right direction? Running now, she stumbled in the shadowy gray light, racing down a dune and colliding head-on with a flock of gulls seeking shelter from the oncoming storm. Brenna's screams pierced the air as the birds flapped about her. It was something straight out of Hitchcock's *The Birds*, she thought—something out of a nightmare. She spun around waving her arms, trying to get clear of the startled birds. She had no idea if she faced the right direction but she raced

blindly forward. Suddenly a light pierced the growing darkness and strong arms scooped her up and
carried her away from the flapping, startled birds.

"You little fool."

Her body shook with fear and it took some moments for her to realize who had rescued her. When
she did, Brenna collapsed gratefully into Jonathan's
arms.

"Here, put this on." Jonathan helped her put on
the fisherman's sweater he had brought with him.
"Of all the dumb stunts to pull."

Exhausted, Brenna leaned against him for support
once more. "Don't scold me, Jonathan," she whispered.

Something in her voice broke through his anger.
"It's all right. You're all right," he murmured, then
muttering an oath he gathered her into his arms and
covered her mouth with his own. His kiss was tender
and reassuring. Finally, he released her. "We've got
to get out of here," he sighed. "It will be coming
down in buckets before we know it."

Brenna nodded. He grasped her hand protectively
and led the way to safety.

"Why did you come here?" he shouted above the
wind.

"I needed to think," she told him honestly. In the
distance Brenna saw the launch. Once they were
safely on board, she would explain about the phone
call. Then she would have her old Jonathan back.
Then they could resume their friendship.

"Have you come to any conclusion . . . about
your phone call?" he asked.

Brenna halted in her tracks. She had been right all

along. It was Clifton's call that had instigated Jonathan's behavior the last several days.

"Have you found that girl yet? This storm is going to break any minute." Brenna could barely make out Monica's silhouetted form but there was no mistaking her voice.

Jonathan switched off the giveaway flashlight. Not now, Monica, he thought.

Brenna was furious. How dare he question her about Clifton when he had flaunted Monica in front of her the entire weekend! And here the singer was again. Brenna felt like a fool.

"Thank you for coming to my rescue, Jonathan," she said, turning to him, "but my personal relationships are just that—personal!" And, tugging her hand from his, she stalked to the boat.

Monica didn't bother to hide her disdain when Brenna entered the cabin. Her expression turned fretful, however, when Jonathan entered. "Do we have to wait out the storm here?"

"Don't worry, Monica. We'll be able to outrun it," he said calmly, starting the motor.

The trip to Rockland passed in deadly silence. Jonathan was intent on handling the launch through the choppy waters while the two women sat restlessly like two caged cats. By the time they reached Rockland, the threat of a major storm was beginning to dissipate. Only a drizzling rain materialized while the main storm was blown out to sea.

"Is everyone all right?" Nathan asked as the quiet trio entered the salon.

"Everything is fine, Nathan," Jonathan said tightly, walking directly toward the bar.

"I'm sorry for any inconvenience I caused," Brenna said, walking over to the worried man.

"You should be," Monica retorted unnecessarily.

Brenna whirled about to face her. Enough was enough!

"Believe it or not, Monica, I really wanted to see Matinicus Island," she defended, barely controlling her anger, "and I did until I dozed off. I had no idea a storm was heading in our direction."

Nathan quickly concurred, his eyes darting from his niece, to Jonathan and back to Brenna. "What's important is that everyone is all right. Now, why don't you three get ready for an early supper," he advised, dismissing them as a parent would dismiss his children after a sibling squabble.

Brenna heeded Nathan's advice, left the salon, ignoring her brooding rescuer who poured himself a glass of brandy, gulping it down with a quick snap of his head.

In the safety of her room, Brenna quickly whipped the bulky fisherman's sweater over her head and threw it in the corner, followed by her damp jeans, sneakers, and socks. God! Was she really such a fool to believe she could beat the odds against an office affair —a *temporary summer* office affair at that. She tossed the rest of her clothes into the hamper and stepped into the glass-enclosed shower, turning the water on full force and as hot as she could bear it.

Perhaps she had been too eager to get involved again, as if the acquisition of a new love could erase the failure of an old one. Perhaps, subconsciously she was too vulnerable and thus blind to Jonathan's faults. But up until the fateful morning Clifton called, she felt her relationship with Jonathan was so right, so mutual and real.

Brenna was mentally exhausted by the time she stepped out of the shower. She was far too drained to deal with her ruined hair. It was easier to twist and anchor it atop her head. She soon realized the last thing she wanted was a full-course meal and more unspoken accusations, especially with Michael and Elaine present. She slipped into her nightgown and robe and, when Godwin knocked on her door an hour later announcing dinner, she asked him to extend her apologies to her host. The events of the day had taken their toll, she told him and since she felt a little feverish—which was the truth—she was going to bed early.

"If it isn't too much trouble, I would appreciate a cup of tea or hot chocolate."

Godwin smiled reassuringly, "No problem, Miz Brenna. I be right back," he said in his lilting island accent.

Brenna plumped up two pillows, then slipped beneath the cold sheet and blanket, pulling the covers up to her waist. All her good intentions to relax and put the day's events behind her were thwarted when her mind involuntarily latched on the kiss she shared with Jonathan on Matinicus Island, where for a brief moment she believed all would be right between Jonathan and her again—once she explained Clifton's call. But she had permitted Monica's unknown and jarring presence to rattle her, throw her off her stride. She had immediately assumed Jonathan was playing games, romancing her with Monica less than a hundred yards away. Now that she was calmer, Brenna had to admit it was possible that Jonathan hadn't asked Monica along for the ride at all. Hadn't the singer taken over all their outings, orchestrating them to her liking?

The knock on her door barely registered when in walked an obviously brooding Jonathan carrying her tray. "I hope this illness is legitimate," he said harshly, placing the tray on the night table. "Otherwise I think you've caused enough melodrama for today. Don't you?" He reached out and touched her fevered forehead. Angered Brenna slipped farther beneath the sheet.

"Satisfied?" she said huffily.

"Yes . . . you do feel warm," he admitted.

"Then thank you for your concern," Brenna said caustically, "but I think what I need now is sleep."

The next morning Brenna learned arrangements had been made for Michael and her to return to Bar Harbor by helicopter without Jonathan who planned to travel to Seal Harbor with Nathan and Monica. Brenna decided then and there that Monica could have the great Jonathan Maxwell with her blessing. She didn't need to be hung up on a man who assumed the worst of her at every opportunity, a man who flaunted another woman in her face and embarrassed her in front of her friends.

Brenna kept to her resolve by keeping herself busy and the first duty on that agenda was locating Clifton and putting an end to any reconciliation ideas he may have been entertaining. That task accomplished, she turned her attention to her work and career. In the daytime she worked on the construction of the model house. At night, she prepared her résumé and typed letters to architectural firms in

New York City, Philadelphia, and Atlanta—three cities she was particularly fond of. By chance Jonathan came across her list. His jaw clenched and unclenched while he scanned the names of prospective employers.

"I know some of these firms personally," he revealed. "If you'd like, I can contact them and put in a good word on your behalf," he offered.

"No thank you. A letter of recommendation would be sufficient." She didn't wish to be beholden to him for more than she had to.

Michael's only comment regarding the strain he suspected Brenna was working under came during a late evening stroll along the beach. "This project won't last forever," he said quietly, tossing a pebble into the surf. "Three more weeks and our work will be over. This summer will be behind us."

Michael's words did not soothe her as he had intended. Instead, Brenna found herself thinking of the first winter's snow, a winter she would not see on Mount Desert Island.

The basket Brenna carried was too full to hold another blueberry, so she popped the last handful of fruit into her mouth. She conjured up a picture of blueberry pies and family reunions in Richmond, Virginia, with generations of Bryants in attendance. Generations from the age of seven to one hundred and one. Generations that fought in both world wars, Korea, and Vietnam too. It was funny how an insignificant thing like a blueberry could trigger such reveries. Recollections of generations of strong, vital, black people who had survived greater disappointments than her lost love.

She felt the sudden urge to run, to run as far and as fast as her legs would permit. To put some distance between herself and her thoughts. But that was wistful foolishness on her part. If she ran, she'd spill her fruit and she didn't want to lose a berry.

For the first time in over a week, Brenna felt she had come to grips with all that had recently transpired in her life. Feeling more lighthearted, she retraced her steps to the house. Reaching the clearing behind the patio, she noticed the kitchen windowsill where she had left two baked shrimp quiche to cool was noticeably empty. Either Michael or Jonathan had returned early. She skipped lightly onto the patio and peeked through the window, hoping to see Michael's cherubic face. She found Jonathan sitting at the kitchen table and, by the looks of one pie plate, he had already eaten two slices of quiche. What to do? Her first reaction was to turn around but where would she go? Back to the woods? She knew that was out of the question but before she could make up her mind, Jonathan glanced up at the door. Caught. Brenna smiled hesitantly and walked in.

"Hello. You're back earlier than I expected." She placed her basket in the sink, turning her back to him.

"I see you've been busy. The quiche is delicious," he said between bites.

"I'm glad you like it." Brenna thought their veiled civility was laughable when she recalled how easy it had once been to speak to him. "I thought the quiche would go well with a salad. Remind me to give you the recipe before I leave."

She kept her back to him, taking her time washing the blueberries, hoping he would finish eating soon and leave, totally unaware of the grimace that crossed his face when she mentioned leaving.

Jonathan's presence was suddenly felt behind her. "Blueberry muffins?" he queried, placing his empty plate on the drainboard.

"No . . . pie." She rinsed off the last of the fruit and placed it in a bowl. "I couldn't find any muffin pans."

Brenna felt the gentle pressure of his hands on her hips and closed her eyes. She had missed this. The comforting closeness. But she wasn't anyone's yo-yo. He couldn't think the worst of her one minute and then turn around and be kind the next. She tensed visibly but Jonathan ignored it, moving closer to her, securely pinning her between himself and the sink. Without moving, he stretched one long arm to the top cabinet and pulled out the pans. "Need any help?" he asked.

"No. No, thank you. I love baking but I can be a bit messy."

Firm lips lightly touched the back of her neck, turning the pit of her stomach to molten longing. "I don't mind messy," he whispered, wrapping his arms around her, beneath her breasts.

This wasn't fair. Brenna sighed. He wasn't being fair. Brenna extricated herself from his embrace, nonchalantly picking up a pan and greasing it methodically with cooking oil. Jonathan picked up the second pan and followed her lead, but the rhythmic motions of his fingers reminded her of his touch on her skin and she shivered. She didn't want to remember.

"Do you have anything planned for the rest of the day? After you bake your muffins, of course."

It wouldn't take long to prepare the muffins, she knew. What excuse could she give that would take up her time for the next five or six hours. It had to be important enough—at the very least believable—to justify turning down any invitation he might offer. Oh, where was Michael when she needed him? The sound of a car door slamming closed gave Brenna hope. Had Michael returned?

"Jonathan! Jonathan!"

But it wasn't Michael's voice they heard. It was Monica's. Oh, well, one excuse was just as good as another.

"We're in the kitchen, Monica," Brenna called out to Jonathan's consternation, judging by the look on his face.

"Just say the word and I'll get rid of her," Jonathan said suddenly.

Brenna turned to face him. How quick he was to dismiss one woman for another, she thought. "Monica's driven from Seal Harbor just to see *you,* Jonathan," she reminded him. "I don't believe she'll simply turn around and leave. Do you?"

Jonathan muttered something Brenna was positive she was better off not hearing clearly.

"Jonathan. What are *you* doing in the kitchen on a nice day like this?" Monica stood in the doorway watching the scenario before her. "Oh, hello, Brenna. Cooking?"

This was the chance Brenna had been waiting for. "I'm going to bake blueberry muffins. But I don't believe I have enough fruit."

Jonathan's hand shot out and he grasped her wrist. "I think you have enough!" He was making it perfectly clear that he didn't want her to leave.

Monica walked to the kitchen sink and looked into the bowl. "I'm afraid I'm not much of a cook, Jonathan, but I would think Brenna would know whether or not she had the right amount of each ingredient."

Reluctantly he released her wrist and Brenna scooped up her empty pail. "I'll just run out and pick some more."

Jonathan watched her through the back window, his eyes never leaving Brenna's fleeing form, as she crossed the patio and clearing, vanishing into the forest. "I think it's time you and I had a little talk, Monica," he said firmly.

CHAPTER EIGHT

"How are you coming along with the boathouse?" Michael stretched lazily, raising his hands above his head. They had been working since nine o'clock and it was now time for lunch.

Surveying her work carefully, Brenna smiled. "Although adding a boathouse wasn't part of the original plan," she sighed, "it's such a small replica compared to the Victorian house that it will be done in time. And, it will complement the main house nicely."

For two weeks Brenna and Michael had worked meticulously on the model Victorian house, which, when restored, would look like a marvelous mansion of old, complete with a well-groomed lawn and landscape. The model house itself was just about complete when Nathan mentioned his negligence in providing a permanent home for his sloop and launch. Jonathan had assured him that two and one-half weeks was plenty of time to work in this addition into the scheme of their original designs and plans. Overnight he had come up with a rough drawing. In two days the final points were added and Brenna was instructed that the construction of the boathouse was her duty. She had to admit that, despite her personal problems with Jonathan, he was an architect of the highest caliber. Both apprentices' respect for the architect's work had grown immensely.

Shifting slightly in her seat, Brenna massaged the back of her neck. The silence of the afternoon was broken by the sound of Jonathan's approaching Jeep. Ever since their confrontation in the kitchen a week ago, Jonathan had been like a bull in a china shop. Brenna still managed to live up to her resolve, maintaining a business acumen, asking questions that pertained to her work alone, never offering more conversation than was necessary. Jonathan was perpetually angry. Even Monica stopped her frequent visitations.

"I think I'll check on lunch," Michael said tentatively.

Brenna couldn't blame Michael for making himself scarce. He was in the unenviable position of watching two people he had grown fond of act like total strangers. There was always a feeling of tension in the air when Brenna and Jonathan were in the same room. More than once he had caught Brenna glancing furtively in Jonathan's direction, a look of bewilderment, loss, and regret on her face. He heard the brusque clipped tone Jonathan used when giving her instructions. The strained civility of the two clouded the entire project. Something had to give and soon.

Jonathan walked into the room and, without looking up, Brenna sensed his presence. He walked to Michael's work area, his eyes passing over the nearly completed Victorian House. Then he walked over to Brenna. He turned the miniature boathouse around, his eyes narrowed slightly, surveying it from all angles. "I know this was a last-minute addition to the project," he told her, "but I expect accurate work all the same. Are you sure you measured this to scale accurately?" he challenged.

Brenna glanced at her work. "I think you'll find everything in order."

"Double-check your figures."

"I've done that already." What did he expect her to do? Take the model apart and start all over.

"Well, do it again!" Sitting in her chair she was at a disadvantage with Jonathan towering over her. He was intimidating and he knew it. But, instead of being frightened, she was furious. How dare he criticize her work? Whatever their personal battles were, she would never compromise her work.

"I've been working on this framework for the last two days. Why didn't you say something before?" Jonathan's gaze softened imperceptibly. But Brenna didn't see it from her seated position. He had once begged her never to be afraid of him. Now he was throwing his weight around intimidatingly. Why? Because she had rebuffed his last overtures in the kitchen. Left him to ply his wiles on a more-than-willing Monica. "Perhaps if you spent less time with outside distractions, you wouldn't have overlooked my supposed ineptitude."

She heard Jonathan's sharp indrawn breath. She didn't see his dark eyes change from soft to brittle hardness. "Correct me if I'm wrong but I'm in charge around here," he snapped. "What *I* say goes. So unless you don't need my recommendation after all, I suggest you check this again." He tossed the model onto the table with a little too much force. But Jonathan was blinded by anger. She knew the model would be damaged before it landed on the table, before she heard the sound of the splitting, splintering model.

It took a few moments for the shock to wear off.

Jonathan closed his eyes, massaging the bridge of his nose. Brenna, stunned by the loss of forty-eight hours of work, was galvanized into action. With one deft motion she rose from her seat. "I think I'll take my lunch now. *If* you don't have any objections." She didn't stop in the kitchen for lunch however. Instead, she hurried to her room, sweeping up her purse and rummaging around in her lingerie drawer for the keys to her Nissan. Her feet flew across the bridge and then she was in her car, scattering gravel and rock under her wheels as she sped away from the house. Away from Jonathan and his accusations. Away from what could have been and what she now had. Distance. Anger. And pain.

She drove through Bar Harbor and across the highway that joined Mount Desert Island to the mainland. Her hands gripped the steering wheel tightly, so tightly her fingers began to cramp. She had only meant to drive until her head cleared. But a few minutes turned into an hour and she soon discovered herself on the outskirts of Ellsworth. In another fifteen minutes she was parked outside Great-Aunt Emmeline's house and standing on the old woman's doorstep.

The door opened. "Brenna! I thought I heard a car pull up. Please come in. Come in." The old woman's eyes sparkled with delight at her unexpected guest. Brenna instantly felt contrite. Although Jonathan had brought her back to visit his great-aunt several times, she had never shown up alone. Em was so kind, Brenna felt she had no right to burden the woman with her problems, especially if the problem was Em's great-nephew.

"Would you like some tea and cookies, dear? I just

baked a fresh batch of applesauce raisin," Em offered, leading her guest to the parlor.

Brenna absentmindedly munched on a cookie, absorbing the room around her, certain this would be the last time she would visit and share Em's company.

"Am I wrong, Brenna, or do you have something on your mind?" Em asked, her fragile fingers raising her cup to her lips.

"No. Nothing's the matter, Em," Brenna lied. "I'm just on my lunch break. I thought I'd drive in to see if you need anything."

"I didn't know my great-nephew was so generous with his lunch hour," the older woman said, her eyes never leaving Brenna's face. "My dear, I thought we were closer than that. Something is wrong, isn't it?"

Unable to avoid her scrutiny and really not wanting to hold in her unhappiness any longer, Brenna blurted out the truth. Aunt Em sat back in her seat, occasionally closing her eyes and nodding as she listened to Brenna's summer tale. When the young woman finished, Em smiled.

"Now I understand why Jonny was so miserable the last time I saw him," she sighed. "But I must say, that he isn't the only one responsible for the mess you two have gotten yourselves in."

Brenna nodded. She had been just as stubborn as Jonathan had been. "Em, what can I do? The summer is almost over and everything has gone so wrong."

Em snorted. "You could tell him the truth," she advised. "Clear the air once and for all."

"That's easier said than done, Em," Brenna confided. "Your great-nephew isn't easy to approach these days." The two women laughed. The tension and pain Brenna had felt eased somewhat.

"When Jonathan was still in grad school he fell in love with a woman who I'm afraid didn't know what love was all about. She was fickle and ended up engaged to a doctor with an established practice. Jonathan didn't even know she was seeing somebody else. You're the first woman Jonathan has shown any interest in in quite some time."

Brenna could imagine Jonathan's pain and disillusionment. She wondered if he had come to the old woman seeking sympathy just as Brenna had come here today.

"Despite your problems with my great-nephew, Brenna, don't throw it away. You two are continually bumping heads because there must be some real feelings between you."

"But what about Monica Weathers?"

Em chuckled. "She's merely a convenient diversion. He's never brought her here."

This news gave Brenna hope.

"Jonathan's like all the Maxwell men—stubborn! It's been up to the women in the family to let them think they've roped us in but sometimes we have to help things along a bit. Swallow our pride a little when they can't. But once they're certain of your devotion, you'll have the most loving man you could have wished for," the elder woman teased suggestively and Brenna, embarrassed, looked at her hands that were clasped in her lap. The old woman's laughter resounded throughout the parlor. "Judging by your reaction I can tell that my great-nephew has shown you his more gentle . . . passionate side already."

It was three o'clock when Brenna declined Em's offer of dinner and headed back toward Bar Harbor. Her talk with Em had made her feel better, made her see the folly of events that had brought her relationship with Jonathan to its present standing. Unfortunately, she had become so involved in their conversation that she had forgotten the time. She hadn't thought of the smashed model boathouse and returning to work at all. When she mentioned to Em that her tardiness has probably dug the chasm between herself and Jonathan wider, the old woman laughed and gave her a hug. "I'm certain Jonathan is more than willing to meet you halfway Brenna. Once you and he *really* talk, I'm certain everything will be resolved. Just remember that his bark is worse than his bite."

As she drove along, Brenna racked her brain for just the right approach to confront Jonathan and initiate their long overdue talk. But nothing came to mind. Lost in thought, she hardly noticed the drizzling rain but automatically turned on the windshield wipers. She was ten miles from the Mount Desert Narrows Bridge when the rain pelted down harder, though not hard enough for her to stop in the town of Bar Harbor until it stopped. Once she left the town behind, a gale wind blew up suddenly and the rain came down in torrents. Brenna put the wipers on full speed, straining to see ahead of her but with the force of the wind came an angry army of dark gray clouds that swallowed up the bright sky in darkness.

She turned on her headlights just in case some other unfortunate person was out in the storm but she had a feeling she was the only one. The journey was torturously slow and she lost track of time as she concentrated on the twisting road before her. She turned on the car's radio for company but only heard static. Finally, unable to see more than a few feet ahead of her on the lightless road, Brenna pulled over to the side to wait out the storm. She stretched herself out across the front seat and turned on the overhead light and heat. There must be some magazine or book she'd left in the car that she could read to pass the time. She was rummaging around in the glove compartment when she thought she felt the car move. Checking the brake, she assured herself her mind must be playing tricks on her. She eased herself into a comfortable position, having retrieved a paperback novel from beneath the front seat when the car lurched again. In an instant she was out the door, the rain pelting her mercilessly. She leaned on the car for support as the gale winds buffeted her about. Walking around to the side of the car, she pulled wet hair out of her eyes. She had parked too close to the gully and her car now leaned precariously. She thought of backing the vehicle out of its present position but she'd probably only succeed in removing the dirt from under the right front wheel faster and plunge head on into the gully. Well, she couldn't stay where she was.

Squashing the panic that was steadily growing within her with each flash of light, each crash of thunder, Brenna figured she couldn't be more than a mile from the house. She struggled against the wind and fought the tree branches that whipped about her. She focused her mind on the warmth of the house and a hot bath, not on her drenched clothing and the chill creeping into her bones. Finally she recognized a familiar sight, the driveway entrance to Jonathan's home. With an elated heart, she trudged along the drive and soon spotted the silhouette of the house.

By the time she reached the bridge, Brenna thought she would never be warm again. Then the front door flew open and a bright light fell upon her. She shielded her eyes from the glare and the light was immediately turned off.

"Brenna!"

She heard her name on the wind and knew she was safe. Strong arms half dragged, half carried her into the house. What a relief not to feel the cold rain or angry wind.

"I'll carry her upstairs," she heard Jonathan murmur to Michael. "You lead the way with the lamp, then call Nathan and Em and let them know she's safe."

Strong but gentle hands brushed the hair from her face and for the first time she was aware of the concerned expressions on both men's faces.

"Jonathan . . . I . . . my car . . . is in the gully by now," she whispered.

"The hell with the car!"

Michael started up the spiral staircase and Jonathan followed with his exhausted bundle who had thankfully put herself in his capable care.

Placing the lamp on her bedside table, Michael left to make his phone calls, using the extra flashlight he carried for guidance.

"All the lights are out," Jonathan informed her. "The backup generator isn't working either."

He placed Brenna gingerly on the bed, then proceeded to take off her shoes. Closing her eyes, Brenna shivered violently. When she opened them again, Jonathan wasn't to be seen in the pale light that shone only on the bed. Yet, although she couldn't see him, she could hear him walking around the room, pulling open drawers. With his penetrating eyes, he could probably see in the dark, she thought.

Jonathan returned to her bedside with several items and proceeded to unbutton her shirt. His intentions clear, Brenna shyly pushed his hands away.

"Don't be difficult Brenna," he commanded. "You're shaking so badly that by the time you got your clothes off you'd already have pneumonia and a slew of other complications."

She knew he was right, but she couldn't squelch her embarrassment just the same. Her hands ceased their protest and she closed her eyes and looked away from him. When he did not make a move to resume his task, Brenna opened her eyes. The look on his face was inscrutable. Without breaking his gaze, he leaned across the bed and lowered the flame until only a flicker of fire indicated the lamp was still lit. In the darkness he gently raised her to a sitting position and removed her soaked shirt and bra. He pushed her back gently onto the bed and with unsteady fingers unsnapped her jeans.

"Raise your hips."

She did as she was told, but before she could be more embarrassed he placed her in a sitting position once more and wrapped a large bath sheet around her. He rubbed her briskly, forcing warmth into her skin, stopping only for a few minutes to take a smaller towel and dry her hair.

"Are you completely dry?" he murmured.

"Yes." He had been very thorough.

Removing the towel from her, he ordered her

arms raised and quickly helped her put on a night-dress. With one arm he lifted her off the bed, while the other pulled back the quilt and sheets. Once she was comfortably settled, he turned the lamp up to its full brightness.

"You get yourself into the damnedest situations," he growled. "How did you ever survive a year abroad on your own?"

Brenna remembered Em's words: *His bark is worse than his bite.* She was touched by his under-standing of her modesty and overwhelmed by his tenderness and his concern. Brenna reached out hesitantly and handed him the smaller towel.

"Your hair . . ."

He sighed, then gave his hair a few brisk obligatory strokes before throwing the towel aside. "Don't worry about me. I'm not the one who looks like a drowned kitten."

She touched his hair and he turned silent. A groan escaped from his throat and he lowered his head to kiss her briefly. "My God, do you know how worried I . . . we all were. Nathan was frantic and Em. Em heard about the fast-approaching storm just after you left." He leaned across her waist, resting his elbow on the bed, cradling his head in the palm of his hand. Casually, with his free hand, he tenderly grazed her lips with his forefinger. The look of concern vanished from his face, replaced by another emotion entirely. When Brenna raised her hand to caress his hair, the quilt fell lower, revealing brown skin through the opened front of her unbuttoned nightdress. Brenna followed his gaze and felt herself flush. She watched him struggle with himself, then surrender to the war within himself. Her breathing came quickly as he kissed her eyelids, murmuring her name before his lips finally caught her mouth in a tentative gentle kiss that threatened to blaze out of control.

Brenna reveled in his arms. It had been so long since he had come near her, since she had permitted him to touch her. Contented, she wrapped her arms about his neck and pulled him down on her and the bed. His fingers caressed her back as his lips released her mouth and traveled down the pulsing throb in her neck, coming to rest in the hollow between her breasts. His hot breath tantalized her skin and, when he brushed his lips over one throbbing peak through the cloth of her gown, she shuddered all the more. His hands didn't cease their wanderings, leaving their imprint everywhere they touched. A knock on the door brought them both back to reality.

"I brought Brenna some brandy," Michael said through the door.

Jonathan pulled her bodice closed, raised the quilt up under her arms, and swiftly walked about the bed and opened the door.

"Is she all right?" Michael looked as concerned as Jonathan had and Brenna managed a weak smile to let him know she would be fine.

"I think she'll be okay. We'll give her the brandy, keep her warm, and hope Nathan's connections can rouse a doctor to look her over tomorrow. No one's coming out in this weather tonight."

"Sleep well, Brenna." Michael squeezed her shoulder fondly, then left the room.

"Here, drink this," Jonathan commanded. He held the back of her head with one hand while he poured the burning liquid down her throat with the other. Brenna gasped as the liquid seared her throat and tried to push the glass away. "Oh, no, you don't. All of it!"

She eyed his amusement over the rim of the glass and gulped it all down. Only a trickle of the brown liquid escaped down her chin. A warmth quickly enveloped her. She could barely keep her eyes open. Jonathan placed the glass on the nightstand and settled her back in bed again. He quickly lowered his head, his tongue flicking out and licking up the trickle of brandy before he invaded her mouth with a slow, earth-shattering kiss that sent her flying into the sweet oblivion of sleep.

"What am I going to do with you?" he whispered huskily. Then he tucked the covers about her once more and turned off the lamp.

CHAPTER NINE

The doctor arrived the following afternoon. Brenna was running a fever and had the chills.

"Let's keep her warm and rested and get plenty of liquids in her," Dr. Nelson instructed. "She's feeling a little achy now. Sounds like the beginnings of the flu."

For the next several days Brenna was of no use to anyone. She drifted in and out of sleep and was thoroughly miserable if she woke to find her night clothes damp from fever. Jonathan kept a close eye on her day and night, and she soon grew accustomed to his handling of her. Except for the first night when they had fallen into one another's arms, he did not touch her again except to insure her comfort. Were it not for the times when his hand shook slightly buttoning or tying up her gowns, she would not have known she affected him at all. Whatever his relationship with Monica was, Brenna was unrepentantly glad to learn that he wasn't totally immune to her.

She was touched by Jonathan's gentleness and patience. She knew she was a terrible patient who hadn't welcomed his ministrations even when she really needed them. She wanted to be left alone. She didn't want him to see her with her hair plastered against her head from fever, her nose running from her cold. She merely wanted to lie in her misery and silently pray for all her illnesses to end.

Slowly, Brenna's strength returned. She was able to keep down the broth and soups Michael brought her in the evenings and the soft-boiled eggs and toast she usually ate for breakfast too. After five days, Brenna was sitting up in bed. Her fever was gone; her limbs no longer ached. She longed to return to work, to rebuild the damaged model boathouse. But every time she voiced her concern to Michael, he told her not to worry. Jonathan had everything under control.

By the seventh day Brenna was definitely restless. She sat in bed flipping through the magazines Jonathan purchased for her, unable to get engrossed in the soap operas that dominated the television. She had fretted over Em's advice for days before speaking to Jonathan about their roller-coaster relationship, but not until she was permitted out of bed. She didn't want any false emotions to get in the way. She didn't want Jonathan's concern for her illness to cloud his mind. If they had been at cross purposes the entire summer, she wanted to know it. Above all, when she explained Clifton's phone call, she desperately wanted him to believe her. She couldn't leave Maine with his thinking she was as unscrupulous as the woman who hurt him long ago.

Brenna toyed with the remote control in the hope that she would find something interesting on the TV when someone knocked on the door.

"Come in." Brenna assumed it was Michael or Jonathan coming to check on her. She was totally surprised when Monica walked in.

"Jonathan asked me to bring these up." She

handed the magazines to Brenna, then took a seat in the chair beside the bed. What was Monica up to, Brenna wondered. She certainly was behaving rather subdued.

"You look like you'll survive," the singer said.

"Yes, thanks to a lot of tender care from Michael and Jonathan, I think the flu is behind me now." Brenna braced herself, certain the woman would make some caustic remark about how much tender care *she* was getting from Jonathan so she was equally surprised when Monica said, "Jonathan was very concerned for your welfare. I envy you."

If she wasn't lying in the center of her bed, Brenna thought she would have fallen on the floor from shock. "You envy me?" Brenna stuttered.

"Well, I never was fortunate to become ill so Jonathan Maxwell could wait on me hand and foot." Monica's laughter filtered through the room. It was genuine without a trace of sarcasm. Brenna was flabbergasted.

"But you do have an advantage over me, Monica. You've known Jonathan much longer."

Monica nodded. "True, longer but not better. Jonathan and I have always been friends even when we first met in college," she revealed. "Oh, I won't say that I didn't have a romantic thought or two about him, way back when, but I was always involved with someone not as dedicated to his work as Jonathan was at the time. And still is." The expression on Brenna's face must have shown her skepticism, for the other woman continued. "I know I probably gave you a different picture of my friendship with Jonathan. But for a while I was pretty confused. Jonathan helped me to straighten things out. It was easier for me to contemplate a romantic summer fling with an old flame than to concentrate on my less-than-soaring singing career."

"But you had a Number-One song a little over a year ago and several others before that. Champagne has established itself in the record industry. You can't possibly think yourself a failure." Surely Monica wasn't blind to her own talents.

Monica laughed. "I forgot. You've been out of the country for over a year. I left Champagne right after our last Number-One song. I thought I could go it on my own. I was wrong. With Champagne, the three of us energized off of one another. We had our routines but every performance was different because we played off one another, did quite a bit of ad-libbing." Monica pulled a pack of cigarettes from her purse and lit one, inhaling deeply. "When I went on my own, it was just me."

The room was quiet for a few moments. Brenna mentally took back every unkind word and thought she had had for the woman. "Jonathan helped me see that a summer fling wasn't really what I wanted. But a career. I don't know if I want to still be one-third of Champagne forever, but we'll be reuniting sometime this winter. Fortunately, my replacement didn't work out."

"And Jonathan helped you see this," Brenna said quietly.

Monica nodded, then laughed. "He said he'd never take advantage of me and get involved. I was trying to hide from one disappointment by fabricating a romance with him." She inhaled on her cigarette again, then crushed it out in a crystal ashtray. "Thank God Jonathan knew me well enough to set me straight. I'm sorry if my presence put a damper on the end of the summer for you." Brenna understood the woman's implication. The woman hoped she hadn't ruined anything between Jonathan and herself.

"No, you didn't put a damper on anything, Monica. I only wish you and I had *really* talked before."

Michael's jaw fell to the floor when he walked into Brenna's room and found the two women chatting effortlessly. "Uhhh . . . Jonathan said you were up here Monica . . . but I thought. That is . . . There's a telephone call for you downstairs," he said obviously flustered. "It's Nathan."

Brenna eased herself under the covers. She kept replaying her conversation with Monica. There was no denying the similarities between the singer and herself. Both had suffered recent disappointments. And though Monica was unaware of that, Jonathan wasn't, for they had discussed it. The difference in their situations was that Jonathan had taken the time to talk to Monica. To help her sort through her confusion. He set Monica straight because he was her friend . . . because he cared about her. Where did that leave Brenna? She was becoming more confused by the minute.

He never took the time to sit down and explain his behavior in Rockland or give an inkling of what his true relationship with Monica was. But why? Unfortunately, Brenna could only conclude Jonathan obviously didn't care enough about her to explain anything. She was just his summer apprentice, destined to leave his Maine paradise in less than two weeks. The gentleness he showed her after the storm was probably instigated from profound relief that she hadn't been injured and guilt that he had upset her so that she had been compelled to race off to Ellsworth to begin with. She also couldn't overlook that since the night of the storm he hadn't touched her, except to see to her comfort, again.

Brenna thought of Em's evaluation of her greatnephew. If he was stubborn, he was only stubborn with her. If he had trouble revealing his true feelings to Brenna, why hadn't he had difficulty setting Monica straight?

There was a light tapping on her bedroom door. "Brenna, are you up? How are you feeling today?"

Brenna buried herself deeper under the sheet and quilt. But didn't say a word. It was Jonathan.

Jonathan stood beside the bed, looking down on Brenna's sleeping form. Monica told him that she and Brenna had had a good conversation, cleared the air on a number of issues, and he had immediately come upstairs to see Brenna, not really knowing what he expected of her. Monica gave no indication that Brenna was taking a nap. Oh well, he would talk to her later.

At the sound of the closed door, Brenna opened her eyes. The dull throb in the area of her heart had returned. Jonathan would never be hers. She knew that now.

It felt good to be out of her nightclothes and into a pair of jeans and sweater. The doctor had stopped by the other day and given her a clean bill of health. But he warned her not to overdue. Brenna combed her hair and put a little makeup under her eyes to conceal the dark shadows, the last vestiges of her illness. Nathan's party was less than six days away. She was eager to get downstairs to look at the model. She knew she'd feel responsible if his celebration was not a total success because she had not fulfilled her duties. Satisfied that she looked presentable, Brenna left her room and hurried down the spiral staircase.

"So you returned to the world of the living," Michael chuckled, when she entered their workroom.

"It's good to be up and around again." They exchanged an affectionate hug. Then, knowing what she longed to see, Michael led her over to the covered model.

"How much remains to be done?" she asked hesitantly.

"Voila!" With a single flourish Michael swept the black silk covering off the models. They were completely finished. The main house stood thirty inches high. The paddle-wheel motif in the railing circled the entire house. The undulating encircling porch decks could be glass-enclosed in the winter and screened-in in the summer. The original pilot house with a bonnet roof atop the central roof was all the more impressive now that a skylight had been added. The structure's deep rust color with startling forest-green accents on the shutters and roof and wheel motif guaranteed that Victorian House would blend into its surroundings all year long. But Brenna kept thinking about the coming winter, when this summer would be just a memory.

"You did a wonderful job, Michael. I'm sorry you had to carry the burden and complete both the main and the boathouse."

Michael cleared his throat and said sheepishly, "I'd like to take the credit for all this, but I can't."

"Jonathan?"

He nodded. "Ever since you became ill, Jonathan worked day and night to complete this."

Brenna sighed. "If it hadn't been for me, neither one of you would have had to keep those long hours."

Michael recovered the model, grabbed their chairs, and beckoned the young woman to join him by the picture window. Seated, Brenna looked out onto the grounds and knew summer was over. There was a distinct look of fall in the scene before her, although it was only the second weekend in September. But the weather had been strange throughout the country this summer. The West Coast climate was hotter than it had been in years, shattering old records. Perhaps Mother Nature had a few surprises for the Northeast. Somehow she felt winter would come early to Maine this year. But not early enough.

She looked at her companion once more. His blue eyes were intent upon her.

"Brenna, even though you weren't down here to help us complete the models," he began, "we still would have had plenty of time to finish them. I didn't work any long hours. Jonathan did, though he didn't need to. But he did," Michael swallowed and looked out into the gurgling creek. "It was as if he were obsessed with its completion. But," he hesitated, "I somehow got the feeling something else was pushing at him."

"What are you trying to say, Michael?"

"I think he worked so hard because of you."

The two looked at one another briefly, but she tore her eyes away first, concentrating on the trees blowing effortlessly in the breeze.

"If he worked hard for me, Michael, it's probably because he felt responsible for antagonizing me the day of the storm," she rationalized, "or because the sooner this project is over, the sooner I'll be out of his life."

Michael snorted disgustedly and swung one leg over the side of his chair. "You can't believe that, can you? Although I've pretty much kept my mouth shut all summer, I do have eyes, you know? I've seen how you both steal glances at the other when you think no one is watching. And I've seen how hard you work together . . . and play. You're good together."

Now it was Brenna's turn to show her disgust. "If we're so good together, why have Jonathan and I been at odds? Why am I having trouble believing anything you've said?" she challenged, not bothering to mention any of the discussion she had with Monica several days earlier. She'd rather Michael believe that she had lost out to stiff competition, than have him know Jonathan had pretended to be involved with Monica in order to keep Brenna at bay. Whatever had flared between them was brief and she concluded Jonathan obviously felt he had made a mistake. And though he might still be physically attracted to her, that still hadn't been enough to break the wall of icy reserve that kept them apart for so long.

"That's easy," Michael sighed, "you're both alike . . . stubborn . . . pigheaded in your own way."

Brenna laughed. "Thanks a lot."

"Any time," Michael smiled.

"So what are we supposed to do until the big party?" she asked, suddenly at a loss for something to do.

"Orders are that our time is our own until the big day." Michael returned to his draftsman's table. "Oh, by the way, here's some mail I've been meaning to give you."

There was a letter from her sister, Celeste, and a postcard from Karen and Gary Smith, another old college chum who had recently married, and a letter from Barclay, Greenfield and Bowen, a reputable Philadelphia architectural firm. Brenna slit open the letter. They wanted to interview her as soon as possible. She could set the date.

"Are you certain that we're free to do as we please until Nathan's party?" she asked Michael.

"Yes, I'm certain. Why?"

But Brenna never answered him. She was already out the door.

After she read her sister's letter, Brenna set her plans in motion. She would go to Philadelphia, if she could arrange an interview in the next few days. Her family knew she had been ill and the easiest way to put her parents' minds at ease regarding their youngest child would be for them to see her. Plus the added inducement of obtaining a job with a good firm near her family should convince anyone that her hastily planned journey was warranted. Only she need know that the real reason she was leaving was that she felt suffocated where she was and confused. She needed to come up for air. She needed to go to Philadelphia and get a proper perspective on her life. Away from Michael and his good intentions. Away from Monica's kindness and revelations. And above all, away from Jonathan Maxwell.

The only person she did feel she could turn to was Nathan. And, true to his word, he was there when she needed him.

"Don't worry about anything, Brenna. I'll make all the arrangements for you. You'll be in Philadelphia by tomorrow afternoon. When's your interview?"

"Wednesday afternoon." Brenna had been fortunate. When she reached the firm, they sounded pleased to hear from her so quickly and were very accommodating. She could have had the interview the very next day, if she wanted it. But Brenna didn't want to impose on Nathan any more than she needed to.

Her third phone call of the afternoon was to Celeste who was thrilled to hear of her sister's imminent arrival and volunteered to pick her up at Philadelphia International Airport.

Brenna was in the middle of packing her garment bag when Michael passed by her open door.

"Going somewhere?" Michael's eyebrow arched; he obviously disapproved.

"The letter is on the dresser," she told him, continuing her packing. "I've got an interview set for the day after tomorrow. Any questions?"

She knew she sounded caustic but Michael's disapproval rankled her. He had no right to judge. Blue eyes met brown ones and whatever Michael originally planned to say, he didn't. His disapproving stare changed to calm dispassion. "Are you going to wait until Jonathan returns?"

"Where is he?" She dreaded his reaction to her plans. Would he disapprove? Or worse, be thankfully gratefully she'd be gone?

"Ellsworth. With Em."

Then he wouldn't be home until late that night. She didn't need to face him and learn his reaction now. She wasn't ready for *that* much honesty. Not yet anyway.

"No. I don't think so. I have connections to make tonight. I'll leave Jonathan a note." She zipped up her garment bag and placed it on the hook behind the door. "Don't worry, Michael. I'll be back. I wouldn't miss the party for anything."

As soon as Jonathan unlocked his front door that night he sensed a sudden foreboding. His eyes settled on the note with her familiar script when he turned on the light. His conversation with his great-aunt had been very illuminating. But perhaps it had come too late. His fingers shook ripping open the envelope. He read it quickly, his eyes skimming over everything except three words: *I'll be back.*

She'd better be, he thought angrily . . . gratefully.

Michael paced up and down the bridge, occasionally leaning over the railing to catch a better look down the roadway. Jonathan had been barely under control during Brenna's absence. When she called Nathan Thursday and told him she missed her connection in New York, Michael thought his employer's leash had snapped.

"What do I have to do? Go down there and bring her back," he had raged, his surprising outburst startling Michael out of his chair. And Jonathan too. But after a few minutes of conversation, Nathan had managed a smile from the embarrassed architect.

Now the only duty Michael had to fulfill was escorting Brenna to the party on time. Michael leaned over the railing and was just about to turn away when a

limousine turned down the roadway. Thank God.
She was here.

Philadelphia had been just what Brenna needed.
The interview had gone extremely well. One of the
partners, Bowen, was vacationing but she had already agreed to another appointment in ten days
when he returned. Being surrounded by her family
helped too. Philadelphia was having an Indian summer and the family had gotten together and had a
barbecue. It was the first time all the Bryant children
had been home since Brenna had gone abroad more
than a year ago. Talking to her family helped her find
the perspective she sought. A year ago she wanted to
complete her studies abroad, return to the States and
find a position as an apprentice with a reputable firm.
Barclay, Greenfield and Bowen could be that firm.
Anything else in her life was secondary. She had
goals. Plans she had set into motion, family who supported her and wished her well. There just wasn't
room in her life for any complications. Summer was
over. But the sight of Michael and the familiar mill
house lodged a lump in her throat, threatening to
destroy all the resolve she had built.

"My God, Brenna, this party is fabulous," Michael
exclaimed. He handed Brenna a glass of champagne
and the two made their way through the sea of people who congregated in the salon and spilled out
through the sliding doors onto the terrace. "I didn't
expect so many people to attend."

"And why not," Brenna laughed. "Nathan Hammond is well-known in many industries. Oh, he made
his money through the music business but his influence stretches into the financial circles and govern-

ment. Or did I imagine seeing several state and national politicians when I crossed the room?"

"No, you didn't imagine it. And I'm certain quite a few notice you too. You really look stunning tonight, Brenna," Michael said gallantly.

"Thank you." Brenna had bought the black beaded gown at her mother's insistence. The Grecian style left one shoulder bare, its floor length skimmed lightly over her curves. Diamond-studded earrings, a present from her parents for her twenty-first birthday, and a small matching pendant necklace graced her throat.

"Brenna. Michael." Dean Washington maneuvered his way through the crowd. Brenna hadn't even known he would be invited.

"Dean Washington. It's so good to see you," she said.

"It's good to see both of you," he responded jovially. "Isn't this wonderful? You and Michael have done the School of Architecture proud, my dear. Nathan's home-to-be is a work of art."

"We had an excellent teacher, Dean," Michael interjected. "I've learned so much from Jonathan during the past three-and-a-half months."

Brenna took another sip of her champagne. If Michael only knew how true those words were.

"You both shouldn't be so modest," the Dean said, moving aside so a member of the catering staff could get past with a tray ladened with aromatic hors d'oeuvres which they all sampled. "I was just speaking with Jonathan. He said he couldn't have gotten the project done without you both."

Brenna forced the lump down in her throat. Jonathan had sung her praises. If only she could believe he meant them. Her eyes skipped lightly over the crowd until they landed on the person she sought. Jonathan looked unbelievably attractive in his stark white shirt, dinner suit, and black bow tie.

"Are you still here with us, Brenna?" Michael said, following the direction of her eyes.

"I'm sorry, my mind was elsewhere," she said honestly, finally greeting Elaine who had joined them. "You're emerald gown is stunning, Elaine. No wonder Michael couldn't wait for us to arrive."

Elaine and Michael exchanged knowing looks. They were a striking couple with their blond good looks but though Michael looked boyishly charming in his dinner clothes, he couldn't compare with the raw masculinity that Jonathan projected.

Brenna faced Jonathan's direction again. He was signaling for them to join him on the terrace. Michael handed their champagne glasses to Elaine, gave her a quick kiss, then led Brenna through the crowd.

"Ladies and gentlemen, friends and colleagues of Nathan Hammond," Jonathan said clearly, "welcome. Tonight you've heard Nathan announce his retirement from the music business. His competitors are probably overjoyed. But let me remind you Nathan plans to retire in Maine six months out of the year. For the other six months it's anybody's guess where Nathan will be . . . or what, he might be involved in." His words were greeted with a round of applause and the tinkling of silverware on glasses. "To insure, however, that he doesn't lose track of his baby, Hammond Records, I'm pleased to introduce you to the new vice president of production, Monica Weathers."

Monica stepped apart from the crowd to acknowledge the applause. Her midnight-blue beaded gown made her look like a star dropped from the heavens. Jonathan gave her a kiss on the cheek and she retreated into the crowd to stand by her uncle.

"I want to thank all of you for your kind praise for the Victorian model house that Nathan hopes to occupy this time next year." More applause. "However, I would be remiss if I didn't give that praise to the two people who put the models together and made this past summer one I'll remember for a long time. My summer apprentices—Brenna Bryant and Michael Hansen."

He motioned the two to join him. The audience burst into more applause which Brenna and Michael accepted gracefully. "These two were of invaluable assistance to me and I eagerly look forward to following their careers." He paused, then added, "Brenna already has the prestigious firm of Barclay, Greenfield and Bowen interested in her talents. As for Michael, I guess I'll be able to follow his career *very* closely because he has agreed to join my firm. I plan to open an office in New York later this year."

Brenna's smile froze on her face. During the entire drive to Seal Harbor, not once had Michael mentioned that Jonathan had offered him a job. Or that he had accepted. Brenna was livid. He should have told her. She would have been prepared. She offered Michael hollow congratulations and amidst the dying applause and mingling crowd excused herself from Jonathan's side.

"Brenna, wait. I want to talk with you," Jonathan whispered.

"Oh, I think you've said it all, Jonathan," she said firmly, vanishing into the throng.

All the determination Brenna had built within herself to handle her brief return to Maine shattered around her like so many broken pieces of glass. She didn't think twice when she bumped into Godwin and asked if she could borrow any available car. "I forgot a gift at the house," she lied.

A litany of all the old accusations and misunderstandings that had plagued Brenna the entire summer echoed in her mind. At first she remembered all the pain. Then she willed herself to think about the good times. What had she wanted to get out of this summer, she asked herself. What had been her original goals: to rest . . . learn . . . and, hopefully, come out of it all with a good recommendation and a job to look forward to.

Almost three out of four—knock wood, if she got the job—isn't bad. A chuckle barely escaped from her throat, before she again felt the swelling lump. No, she couldn't say the summer had been restful. At times, it had been idyllic, and yes, she dare say romantic. At least she had a taste of the romance she had always believed, deep down inside, did exist and could exist between a man and a woman. At least she knew for certain that her broken engagement had been a blessing in disguise. And, she was happy for Michael. And Jonathan too.

Her mind turned back to lazy evenings reading a popular paperback while the two men played chess.

The honk of an oncoming car jarred Brenna to attention. "Put your lights on," the driver bellowed. She did as she was told, surprised that she hadn't reached the entrance to the house. A bubble of laughter erupted the silence. She'd been so engrossed in her thoughts, she had driven past the entrance. At least, three miles past. She turned the car around, the lump in her throat gone and forgotten.

Brenna shut off the ignition and let the silence of the night engulf her. It was twilight but the house was no less imposing. No less beautiful. The flowing stream below and the wind were subtle accompaniments to the click of her heels as she crossed the bridge. She would walk along the pebbled beach one last time and leave early the next morning. She probably wouldn't get the chance to say good-bye to Michael. But for some reason she believed he'd understand. She'd leave him one of her famous notes. She walked slowly around the house to the patio.

"Where have you been?"

The receding lump leaped to her throat. Her heart palpitated wildly with fright. She whirled about, seeing the glowing embers of his cigarette. Jonathan had scared her half to death! What the devil was he doing sitting in the dark?

"I went for a drive, if you must know. Not that it's any of your business," she added, resuming her walk toward the path that led to the sea. "I don't work for you any longer."

She heard his chair scrape back on the patio. She sprinted down the path. Not easy to do in heels.

"Brenna. Come back here!"

But she was never coming back, she thought hysterically. She knew that. Why couldn't Jonathan just leave it alone? Just as he did all summer long. She didn't need to hear the reasons behind his rejection tonight, if that's what he had in mind. Her high heels were not the appropriate footwear for walking on pebbles. She knew she was behaving irrationally but she really didn't need a scene. Hot tears formed in her eyes when she accepted the helplessness of the situation. If she had hoped not to have to face Jonathan again, she should have stayed in Philadelphia. A strong hand gripped her arm and stopped her flight.

"God," he groaned, "have I finally driven you from me completely?"

His hold on her lessened. But his words held her locked in his grip. What was he saying?

In the full moonlight she read the distress in his eyes.

"You never did lie to me about Clifton from the very beginning. I know that now. I think I always did. It was just the possibility of being cuckold again that infuriated me." His eyes were dark bottomless pools. She was afraid to believe this was truly happening to her. She was afraid she had walked into a magical night and as soon as she batted an eyelash the vision she thought was Jonathan would be gone. She reached out a hand, placing it beneath the opening of his shirt. His bow tie hung limply down his shirt. His heated flesh beneath her fingertips reaffirmed him flesh and blood.

"You didn't drive me away, Jonathan. I did that," she murmured.

Brenna moved closer into the circle of his arms, lifting her face invitingly for his kiss. Their lips met with a burning hunger that threatened to consume them where they stood.

"No, love," he murmured, breaking off their kiss. "I was wrong about Clifton and I was wrong to surprise you with Michael's announcement." He cupped her face between his hands. They stared unflinchingly into one another's eyes. "But you had me so tied up in knots and confused."

"Join the club," she teased, nibbling on his lower lip.

"No, Brenna, I'm serious," he continued. "The first day we met I thought you the most beautiful woman I'd ever met. I don't know what I expected from 'Brenna Bryant,' the builder of the colonial home, but you took my breath away. When I thought you were engaged," he agonized, "I was furious. When you met Em and you told me about Clifton I believed you. It was that damn phone call that made me feel you had lied to me," he sighed. "And I used Monica to get back at you. I'm sorry."

"Jonathan I . . ."

"No, let me finish, Brenna." He took off his jacket and wrapped it around her shoulders. "The night of the storm I was positive I'd been wrong about you. When Monica told me she had talked to you and explained our friendship, I decided not to stick *my* neck out but wait and see what you did instead."

"I didn't do anything, Jonathan, because I was positive that the reason you wanted me to believe you and Monica had a relationship wasn't simply because of Clifton, but because you really didn't have any serious interest in me."

Jonathan's laughter reverberated around them. "Brenna, if you only knew how much serious interest I had. I went to Em's the day you *ran* to Philadelphia, because I finally realized I'd been so concerned for your health that I never did question Em about your visit."

"Poor Em. Subjected to your third degree," Brenna retorted, permitting him to lead her to a boulder which he leaned against, drawing her into his arms.

"Poor Em, nothing. She had a few choice words for me!"

Brenna laughed. "And she told me she had a few choice words for you—later—once we cleared everything up. Which was exactly what I planned to do tonight but you were gone." His arms tightened, nearly taking her breath away; then he relaxed his hold. "I could have strangled you, when you said you missed your plane. I thought you weren't coming back at all. That it was just an excuse."

"I thought about not returning, Jonathan. But I'm no coward. Well, at least," she corrected, "not until tonight."

"I don't know what possessed me to go ahead with the announcements before I talked to you. But you were late arriving and I was angry . . . and . . ."

It was Brenna's turn to laugh now. "Oh, Jonathan. And you said I thought too much."

Jonathan took her words as an invitation and kissed her again. A groan escaped from deep within his throat when his probing tongue met hers in search of his.

"Jonathan," Brenna murmured after a time.

"Hmmm . . ."

". . . I want you."

Jonathan stiffened. "Are you sure?" he asked, looking down at her. The smile on her face and light in her eyes was all he needed to see.

"That's wonderful! I offered Michael a position with my firm in New York. But for you," he said soberly, "I offer a lifetime with me . . . here in Maine."

His dark gaze flickered over her and she trembled at the smoldering look in his eyes. He kissed the trail of salt tears that unexpectedly spilled from her eyes.

She smiled coyishly. "Are you throwing in a few side trips to New York too?" she teased breathlessly.

"Uh huh . . . maybe even a partnership with the firm one day." He breathed against the sensitive cord in her neck. "But for now I have another partnership in mind . . . as my friend . . . lover." He punctuated each word with a kiss. "Most importantly as my wife. Interested?"

"It sounds like the type of position I've been waiting for all my life."

Jonathan smiled and lowered his head. Their lips sealed their love as arctic terns flew overhead en route to their winter home.